Mood Lightning

for Ling Choon Hiong
who is steadfastly swayed by impulse,
that of love

the first IMAGINAL PRESS book

Published by **Imaginal Press** 2004

Email: luminousword@lycos.com

National Library of Australia
Cataloguing in Publication data:

Mood Lightning: an anthology

ISBN 0 9756773 0 6

1.Literature - Collections. I. Ten, Ch'in Ü

808.8

Design by Dhyan Tao-Li Ho
Cover painting by Peter Cameron
Printed and bound by Southwood Press

Mood Lightning

an anthology edited by Ten Ch'in Ü

"The word is luminous."

Ista Chuang-yang Ho
when asked whether the ghost
he saw was a glow-in-the-dark one

IMAGINAL PRESS

Acknowledgements

Some of the contributions in the collection have appeared in the following publications:

A Carnival of Poets ed. Mariso Cano, Jackson Press
A Crack in the Wall
A Writing Unexpected, Ginninderra Press
Banipal (spring 1999)
Five Live, Live Poets Press
Hope in Progress, Taurus Press
Kardoorair Broadsheet
Made in Public, Taurus Press
Misplaced Heart, Five Islands Press
New Humanist
Open Boat, Live Poets Press
Ouyang Yu: New and Selected Poems, Salt Publishing
Poetry and Audience
Spectrum
Stories of the Feet, Five Islands Press
The Night, the Song and Tomorrow, Burg Press
Times Literary Supplement
Tirra Lirra
You Chase after Your Likeness, Round Table Publications

Clarissa C. Burt's translations of *Wadih Sa'adeh*'s work were first published in Edebiyat (Vol 14, 2003), Taylor and Francis. Some editorial changes were made for this book. Wadih's work also appears at http://www.geocities.com/wadih2

Any performance or public reading of *Bogdan Koca*'s 'Lexes', 'Reality No 6' or 'Biding Time' must first obtain permission from the author (bogdan@sat.org.au).

Some of the poems and prose in this collection were first presented in evenings of poetry and discussion I held at **Rudolf Steiner House**, 307 Sussex St in Sydney, between April 2002 and November 2003. *Norma Blackwood* graciously made available the use of the rooms and *John Pater* kindly accommodated some of these gatherings in his Tuesday schedule.

Danny Gardner frequently encouraged and gave critical feedback at various stages of the project. *Susan Haris* and *Wadih Sa'adeh* instantly understood and trusted the impulse. *Peter Cameron* allowed the use of his painting for the cover and, with such warmth, also donated a painting to help the self-publishing venture.

John Weerden and *Ryan Joo* deftly conjured away a few pre-production wrinkles. *Felicity Daphné Baldry* gallantly undertook to check a hundred pages and *Hari Ho* dropped a couple of printing hints.

The name of the anthology came in a flash, sparked from the title of John's poem 'Moon Lighting'. Titles of the first eight segments come from poems by Danny, *Pat Pillai, Jorie Manefield Ryan, Brook Emery, Martin Langford* and myself with Pat and Danny providing two each. The ninth is the title of Peter's recent exhibition.

Ron Vaisey was instrumental in christening our Press *Imaginal*; earlier contenders 'Garlic' and 'Ouroboros' might have proved, respectively, over odorous or more than a mouthful.
David Wansbrough thoughtfully placed the first orders.

My son *Dhyan Tao-Li* provided invaluable computer instruction and service. Dhyan designed the cover and was a source of good humour throughout. His creative enterprise informs this book.

Ten Ch'in Ü

Contents

eager clay

"Whatever the unborn and the dead men know, they cannot know the beauty, the marvel of being alive in the flesh. The dead may look after the afterwards. But the magnificent here and now of life in the flesh is ours, and ours alone, and ours only for a time."

D.H.Lawrence
'Apocalypse'

A Response to Light

I ask the dawn
not to wake you.
I ask the dawn
to climb the ladder
as the rose breathes.

Shawki Moslemani
Translated from the Arabic **Where the Wolf is**
by *Noel Abdulahad and Raghid Nahhas*

Braille Cobwebs

the land it is called
the painting is called the land
white ledges batten down the flatness of it
ridges of scraped limestone   without fences
without eyes

here she returns each morning
to sit before sunrise touching salt
until her ears discern changes in the surface of the ocean

slow tracers of ink connect
bloom in pools beyond the tidemark

Pat Pillai

Morning

I awake from dreams
into my sunlit room.
The house, here, where it was.
The children still asleep.
The dog, outside, to be let in.
Birds in the trees.
Garden, sky, world, also awake.

Ten Ch'in Ü

Tea gardens 7am

still river
pelicans preen
on white mooring posts

mangrove shadows flicker

early walkers and cyclists
hardly rate

it's seagulls' and magpies' cries
that cut the air

a boat's radio
a grandmother's instructions to her boy
as they glide past

and the parade of four-wheel drivers
on their journey to the paper shop
as the day heats up

Pip Griffin

Hunter Gatherer

My man loves going to the markets –
a dog with ten tails
when he returns home
with his loot:

a case of tomatoes
box of lettuce
sack of carrots
five cabbages
two or three pineapples
eight capsicum
cucumbers by the dozen
and a carton of overripe figs going cheap.

There's only the two of us
and our two fridges.
He bought the second one
from a delicatessen
going out of business.
Even when the delivery men
took the backdoor off
it wouldn't fit in the house.
Just as well:
it makes a noise
like the digestive system of a dinosaur.

Instead of writing poems
I've become a one-woman preserving factory
as I fill jars with sauerkraut
dry figs in a slow oven
pickle cucumbers
invent recipes for tomato preserves.

Once going overseas

on an early flight
(and planning an early night)

I was faced with a case of eggplant
to slice, salt, grill in a slow oven
before spooning into large jars
filled with olive oil –
finished
just before the taxi arrived.

Now the murky jars
lurk at the back of the fridge
beside the pickled cabbage,
cucumbers,
tomatoes.

It could be worse.
In a former life
he brought home
a woolly mammoth.

Hilarie Lindsay

Take Two

If your neighbour asks for
a lemon from your tree
give her two
just in case
one is a lemon.

Ten Ch'in Ü

The Ordinary Order of Things

Lovely is the clacking of knitters,
the chatter and clicking of needles,
the looping and hooking,
locking and linking its language:
hold your hands out as the skein
winds down to balls,
with knit one, purl one, drop one,
cast one, slip one.
Stories and wool are yarns.
And grandmas' gossiping banter
as rheumatic fingers think
through knitting needles
independent of the talk.
What wisdom is woven in patterns:
knitted chains twisted from the shoulder
to wrist and ribbed cuffs.
A boy's jumper will have
interlocking lemniscates
flowing down his spine.
Knit one, purl one, cast off the row.
In knitting life's threads flows.

Dig the earth and plant a word.
Sounds from the soil taste sweet on the tongue.
Sage, lovage, fennel,
borage, peppermint, dill,
lettuce, cabbage, basil,
onion and chives, parsley, spinach,
rosehips, nasturtiums, star anise,
cardamom, ginger, angelica,
caraway, marjoram, tarragon, coriander.
And thyme.
And the weather and the seasons,
the sun and the moon tides,

and the pregnant autumn.
And the tilling, dibbling, seed sowing,
waiting, weeding, plucking and eating.
All part of the dancing rhythm of life.

Near Solnechnogorsk at an outdoor table,
with frothy beer and crusty bread,
peasants gather round the great *grande dame*
of the village collective
(who in her day had bashed Germans).
Now she comforts a baby girl
who gums her knotty knuckle,
until a mother unbuttons
her full blouse and takes the child to suckle.
Little hands squeeze and knead the breast
and her tiny feet
pulsate against the palm
of mum's hand.
A kid digs spreading dust on feet
with a whittled toy spade.
"Soon," chuckles great-gran.
And the aunties laugh
and the cosmos turns.
"Ah" outbreathes the world,
"men" inbreathes the earth.
"Amen."
That is the way of it.
The dance. So be it.

David Wansbrough

Nursery Rhymes

The perfect little poems known as nursery rhymes really exercise the organs of speech. The baby held to his mother's breast already has the beginnings of speech when he opens his mouth wide to engulf the areola, flattens the nipple with his gums and then pushes it up to the palate with the tongue.

(This is a very different process from chomping with the gums on a teat from a bottle when the milk caught between the teat and the hole is sucked and squirts to the throat. The babe must then reject the teat to break the vacuum, whereas the breast-fed child rhythmically enters into a continuous process.)

It is wonderful to see a baby using the entire body to express contentment when drinking: the feet pulsate against the mother's hands. The baby drinks as a totality. The tongue, lips and palate and throat move in different sequences, but form a totality in co-ordinated movement. This is a mysterious and tender preparation for speech. The process of sucking and drinking is preliminary to articulation. As his dome-like head rests against his mother's chest he hears her familiar heart rhythms which change with different emotions: skipping more quickly with expectation and then more steadily with calm contentment. Sometimes mum and baby blush at the same time as they look into each other's eyes. This is a most subtle communication.

Speech will later express the great expanses of soul moods.

Just as a baby drinks with his whole being, a truly human person speaks with his wholeness, from the depths of his soul.

David Wansbrough in his August 2004 lecture on Nursery Rhymes at Rudolf Steiner House in Sydney

Good Morning, Tub

I lay there in the tub this morning.
Good Morning, Tub, said I,
a lovely day: the sun all a-shine
much for us to resolve this day.

It's a weekend morning, Tub,
not like a workday morning.
Then it's scrub, dress, rush, no fun.
Time this morning Tub, *Time...*

A chance here to dream,
to think through the issues of our day,
to decide what's best for us
and what we tell the world to do.

There is FAI and One-Tel,
but not much we can do there, Tub:
the investigations and commissions
are well and truly under way.

Children overboard and refugees,
something needed there, Tub;
the navy, pollies and the public service
are smelling a little here, Tub.

We could string up Admiral Barrie
with the Minister for Defence,
and all the public servants
that have scarred too deep,
too deep, Tub, our country's soul.

Water is getting cold, Tub,
and not a single good resolve
have we made as yet this day.
And there is still me and you to go
and all the rest of us.

There is of course the barbecue
where the family will come together.
Victoria's new friend to be there:
fifteen of us. The only one he knows

is Victoria. We did warn her.
John is taking bets that he
will not stay the day right through.
What do you think, Tub, we should do?

Extra hot water, Tub,
There is much, much more for us;
there's the new law that is trying
to put us all in jail

if we tell about the government,
not only is it two years behind for us
it's two years for the journo too.
Not good that one Tub, not good at all.

There is the Governor-General, Tub,
and now the Catholic Archbishop,
they did not tell, nor did any clergy.
Why do good men, Tub, not speak out?

Water is cold, Tub, water is cold;
we have solved not a thing
and it is time to go. To go.
Still, it has been my joy today

to share these thoughts with you
working through the problems
of our world. Goodbye for now, Tub.
Goodbye for now.

Peter Bowden

Midsummer Song

There are days when the sunlight
streams paths, doors and windows
over silence and rumours of the hour.

Days when the breeze blows as if
certain gods or goddesses were still breathing
within us.

Days when the smaller of the things
speaks out the *asombrous*
the glory of being alive.

Days like this.

Mario Licon Cabrera

"Poetry? It's part of my body."
Assad Cina when asked if he was still writing poetry.

"I am polyamorous."
Antares of Magick River, Kuala Kubu Baru, Malaysia

Global Warming and a Bronte Beach Morning

It's like leaving the trenches
- from one bloke about to dive in
who's young enough to know nothing of terror or the torn.
Like having sex again
says the woman, surprising herself
with a salt-cured truth.

Midwinter, hair-shook droplets lunge toward the sun.
Lawnmowers share distressed gossip
as CO_2- green breaks out.
This fluorescent season,
flowers bloom then elope.
Sand practises against the waves
to become the bottom of some new harbour.

Icebergs send postcards to four-wheel drives,
accept the invitation north
because being liquid is convenient and fast.

Power stations share a smoke,
write haikus on their press releases.

Someone plans fibreglass hulls under Pacific atolls,
sails tied on palms.
Give natives funny hats
then set tourists to graze
through the low-wage serviced holidays.

IMF requires (naturally)
a floating exchange rate.

The answer is always more.

At around waist level you pause, then make a full dive.
Christ, that water's cold!
Yeah, but we're swimming in July.

Les Wicks

"Sex is okay but it is not as good as the real thing."
Yuri at a farewell dinner during dessert

"Sex? Who are they?"
Two-year-old

At the Gymea Bay Naturalists' Club
we danced for hours at the Nude Year's Eve Party,
swooned at the *stroke* of midnight.

Les Wicks

"I am Telly. Turn me on."
Telly Nakhdjavani-Hall

e e cummings cockatoos

glittering
a white shriek raga
rackets over
nodding lucerne

then like unto
a screech
descending
soundcauterised
through this
ambient-raging afternoon

the cockatoos alight
upon a skeletontree

draggle flap
flickersettle

white full stops

Bill Tibben

Ellington 1927

The faun comes in from the jungle.
No one around. He unslings the piano
from his shoulder and sets it down where
it paws the ground nervously.

A personage from Miró blows a tree.
He is the tree. It dances. Voices rush
out over the water, brake like skidding ducks
among the reeds.

A dog's bark knocks at the foothills. Pan, god of jazz,
drops by. Cool gales shall sometime hit the fan.
Far off a scurrying wind
stirs music pages down a lost arcade.

John Miles

"Pop goes the easel."
Christopher Bodame

"She is the sister of my two fingers."
Anis Ghanem explaining why he still has a cigarette
in his hand and hasn't given up smoking.

Looking Back Down the Road
(loosely after Rimbaud's 'Ma Bohème' and 'Au Cabaret Vert')

1. *Taking Off*

Those days, I'd split without a second's thought. Hit the road.
Just take off. At seventeen, I'd tramp for miles, hitch a ride
no place special. Leather jacket like a scarred second hide.
Signposts for sonnets, truckers' long-load tales for odes.

Service stations, greasy spoons, thumbing cars, cars, cars.
Wind finding new holes in the knees and arse of my strides.
Blacktop, humming rubber, Autobahn-piste-strada.
Crashed out dead in graveyards, dossing under skidding stars.

Sat at the roadside, under creaking trees, the huge race
of clouds. September nights, dew sparkling my face.
Swigging lager from a stolen can: clean, cold, sharp,

conjuring up visions from shadows. Hidden in secret places,
I'd twist feet up close to my heart, pluck the laces
of my wounded boots, entire body tuned to *Harp.*

2. At The Green Café, 5pm

A full week on back roads, dusty mountain tracks.
Old Chinese canvas shoes were shagged-out shreds.
I hobbled into this one-camel town, back
of beyond, saw the green sign, smelled fresh baked bread.

Splashed face at the pipe, dragged fingers through hair.
Inside, this girl looked up, surprised, cracked me a smile,
flicked a rag over the green oilcloth, dusted off a chair.
I stretched my legs out, took in the shiny painted tiles.

She looked good around the eyes, not shy at any rate.
Fetched me slabs of bread, butter, thick folds
of home-smoked ham on a brightly-coloured plate.

Pink and white, delicious, garlicky. For something cold,
she foamed up this huge mug. Getting too late
for the border, a quirky ray of sun turning beer to gold.

Cliff Forshaw

The Source
(after Courbet)

Angophoras fold down

evergreens gaze heavy lidded at the scatter of winnowed siftings
bright on pavement petticoats

gravel scours the washout back to eager clay
and, nothing shy
earth accepts the ecstasy of flood

my umbrella does nothing to protect me

Pat Pillai

"Anyone who has made love knows body and soul are not separate."
John Weerden

Greece - Day Two

You've arrived at Pereas.

Forget the ruins, forget Athena.
Take a bus towards Katos Assos.
Get off around midnight.
Let the moon be your guide
And find a lemon grove to sleep in.

Get up at first light
Before Spiro, the farmer, does his rounds.
Follow the old man along the dusty road
Past the peasants burning brush and the noisy goats.
No matter that the village shopkeeper with the bum eye
Cannot understand you.
Forget the flavoured yoghurt and buy the warm, iced coffee.
Stop outside the Orthodox Church
And acknowledge the certitude
Of mourners in black at morning Mass,
Holding lit candles in the sunshine.

Head on then, past the still houses in the heat
Till you find the unassuming beach.
Never mind the hard little stones,
Open your body to the Aegean's green embrace.
Now your hair is stiff with brine,
Go down to the taverna for fish and tomato salad.
Try the ouzo but take plenty of water.
Pursue Mouskouri maybe, in songs to the wheeling stars.

The next day go up into the pines above the bay.
You may even come across Pan,
Reciting the politics of love
To his band of horny satyrs.

Sooner or later you'll stumble on a wine festival.
Get pissed in honour of Bacchus and Zeus,
To the crazy, trembling bouzoukis
And the young men dancing.

The morning after, you swear you surprise Odysseus,
Under the misconception that history could be repeated,
Landing his boat on the grey-dawn tide,
Overflowing with theatrical woe
And demented ravings about the Sirens.
You smile, thinking Penelope is not such a good love anymore,
But you will have to go home too.
Where you are the stranger now
Shedding your myths upon chance acquaintances…
Feeling Aphrodite's horned…fin, was it?
Stiffening in your coat pocket.

And your back is turned when the photograph is taken.

Danny Gardner

Death leant over me
with a kiss on her lips
as I in the darkness of birth
fumbled at her breast.

Christopher Bodame

Once More with Feeling

She needs a diagram
to place the diaphragm.
The pill makes her quite ill.
She can't condone the condom.
Don't even mention
mucus measurement.
Coitus interruptus isn't quite
her idea of an interesting outing.
She takes such exception
to contraception
that, as expected,
she's expecting
again.

Ten Ch'in Ü

The Bottom Line

I lie on my side   knees drawn up
gaze at a print of *Blue Poles*
while the doctor
sticks a light up my backside.

I enjoyed looking at *Blue Poles*.
I hope the doctor had a nice view.

Hilarie Lindsay

my grandmother said

"Don't point a finger at the moon,"
my grandmother said,
"or it will shave off your ears
as you lie in bed
and unawake."
My fingers trace the pretty shells
not shrunken through the years.

Every then and then
she grew fierce about the sun,
"Don't let the dragon swallow it.
Clap the pots and pans together
before the days are done."
There have been no pitch black days
when no sun shone.
My grandmother won.

When the monsoon wind
pounced into our garden
flapping clothes and clinging hair
"Go indoors, it's an ill wind," she'd say.
We would stay
to pluck
the field of dragonflies
that rode the air.

Dominque Yap

Sing -
I give you the horse.

Shawki Moslemani
Translated from the Arabic **Papers of Solitude**
by *Raghid Nahhas* and *Noel Abdulahad*

dust and eucalypt

"Perception is not the inward reception of something that is already formed, already finished; it cannot be, because the body is living, changing, becoming, not already finished. Perception is thus a genesis rather than a conclusion; it is the opening into the world as becoming. Relationship as a triad with the world as the third, then, is not something that one has or even something that one is in, but a coming-to-be together. A relationship is always a genesis, an advent, an opening, something always at its beginning rather than an event."

Robert Sardello
'Love and the World'

The history of the cosmos
is the history of the struggle of becoming.

DHLawrence
'God is born', Selected Poems

The Horse Man

We were walking down a dirt track
When we saw the white horse in a small paddock
So still it was hardly there.
My friend bent down and pulled some grass
And the horse's tail began to move.
Then we felt the moist mouth on our hands,
His dark watery eyes studying us.
A moment almost unnoticed rescued us from ourselves.

Margaret Smith

Buddhist Banksias

Waiting patiently in the autumn light
Merging on winter
Rustic red over saffron robes
Like sitting lamas in solitary prayer
Yet all chanting as one
Their rhythmic tone enhanced by the rising Sun.
Out on the silvered green leaves of waiting destiny
Silence breathes their sensitive meditation
- In silent devotion -
'Understanding
In the Between.'

Susan Whitehead

The Horses

I first heard English spoken in my third year.
Till then I listened to and responded to Dutch from that watery landscape. Dutch words came to me like oversized wooden contraptions hewn from wild timbers, wheeled across dunes and polders by pirates and painters toward the next windmill.

English words are like domesticated animals, like Hereford bulls, Port Phillip Bays or Oxford Streets, and seemed trained like musical instruments to mesmerise the landscape which they have conquered.

Those which cannot be trained are suppressed or quarantined on arrival, detained, deported or sunk out at sea and when they do survive, seek the company of pirates and dancers, and maybe, if they are lucky, poets.

My parents were like wild contraptions and wheeled across the world's oceans. We kids were like appendages hanging off the bulkhead, scratching the duco, easily broken.

We were migrating to Australia. A Great South Land we knew nothing about. A place where Dutch was not spoken. But where domestication was a lifestyle – a Rainbow snake charmer with a dead snake in a basket.

My parents wanted to be domesticated.
They wanted their children to be trained. They were free to choose any basket. We struggled to make music, to articulate sounds, embrace the spirit of a new language in a new landscape.

And this presented us with a problem. Where was our trainer? Who was our charmer? Who was to show us how to captivate a landscape? Words is one thing but to mesmerise a landscape – that requires insight and technique. A challenge to say the least. When all you've ever known is windmills and pirates.

I grew up as suspicious of the English Language as it appeared suspicious of me. I desperately needed a trainer. If this was a horse race I'd fallen at the start, yet continuing to race wouldn't guarantee domestication let alone a charming lifestyle.

At best I might bring up the rear of the field and be described, if at all, as honest but lacking personality and technique.
"Better take up with the wild bush horses," they might have said.

So imagine the arrogance when I chose poetry as a vehicle. And then the conceit of performance poetry. Without personality and any charm to speak of, I'd have to be mad. But I'm here aren't I?

I'm entering the home straight. There's still a couple of hundred metres to go though with instincts programmed for flight rather than fantasy, it's still pretty tricky.

It's just that I've been training myself at open mikes for nearly twenty years and though my oration seems no better today than it did then, my knees don't knock so heavily.

Yet madness remains a constant for without technique, a garrulous wit, devilish skill or sophisticated nuance, it's a fingertip act dragging the listener along the road to my next windmill.

Perhaps I'm destined to join those wild bush horses running the back paddocks up the dry gullies over the stony rises.
'Cause I can still cobble together some attitude.

Because I have words, hard-won words, undomesticated and feral, out of art and into talent galloping down my own home straight and I'm in pretty good shape.

Ray Wittenberg

Currawongs

Choristers of day and night
and dressed for both, you carve
a scalloped pattern in the air
between the treetops just a rung
below the ravens.

Your all-seeing eyes detect the
scrub's transgressions as with wig
and gown you police its common law,
chasing infanticidal ravens
with parental wrath

Or hangdog, with your partner,
in headlong comic flight from a
diminutive demented mynah that
found an empty nest while you nearby
crammed your youngster's craw.

Last to retire, save for a screeching
rainbow lorikeet evicted from
its Norfolk Island tenement, and first
to hail the silvery eastern glimmer,
your rich contralto

is the leitmotiv that binds
the forest's acts together in a
unity of sound that rises to the
peaks of ecstasy and falls into the
valleys of despair.

When I observe you catapult full-throated
from incensed pittosporum, I marvel
that the first white settlers said our land
was where the flowers don't smell
and the birds don't sing.

David Tribe

The Instant

What is love?
Some love is conscious action
for when old enmity is faced
it becomes the basis
for truer friendship.
And when in a flash
another's fault is found
in us and we take theirs
to share, we are suddenly
in the instant, freer.
And in that suddenness
we sense behind life
a glimpsed sustaining love.

When the dingo
dips his muzzle in a creature's viscera
he himself is food for fleas
and insidious liver flukes.
But even so
the instant is placed in a context,
into the woven pattern of life,
and love.

A man with the sun behind him
who faces far-off showers,
If his line of sight and the trick of the light
rays at only 42° (not 43 or more)
and the angle of the direction
of the rain again is 42°
he finds obliquely that a rainbow
arches *just for him.*

A bumblebee,
hairy heavy pollen laden
hovers over the hive
then lands and dances
the bees' dance of flown distances
of flowers found in fields and forests.

When the didgeridoo drones,
sparks electrically leap in the earth
from rock to crystal
and on the surface
insects collectively for miles
click and thrum in unison.

When boys look down at a billabong
from boulders and laugh and leap
and hug their knees and bomb,
the water rises and the rings ripple
past banks and flow widely
into the world with rough sweet life.

A milk-full baby
chortles lying on her back,
looks at her hands
as distant things
and sings the vowels purely
ah aa ee ii ooh ooou
And the world hums
with love.

If you don't believe me,
look at the banksias!

David Wansbrough

Writing Lyrics for *Monk's Mood*

I was asked to contribute to a discussion on the creative processes involved in writing poetry. Since many of my pieces are more-or-less topical satire or involve a clear line of narrative or at least anecdote, I felt that the processes involved were not particularly interesting – you had a topic, idea or story, a fairly clear idea of how to develop the poem, and you executed it as best you could. Not so simple or straightforward really, and not without interest in the detail, but something I didn't feel like spending my time on, since I felt that I knew many of the answers before I started.

I chose instead a more atypical piece where I had very little idea of what direction the poem would take before I started, where I felt no responsibility to be coherent (since I knew of only one person, a jazz fan and ex-musician, likely to know the tune and appreciate what I was trying to do). I was also writing lyrics for a tune (not even a song as intended by the composer). Songs can get away with all sorts of bizarre and enigmatic lyrics. I felt totally free to abandon myself to the process and let it take me where it chose. It is not surprising, then that the project was fuelled by unconscious and half-conscious impulses such as occur less frequently in much of my work. These seemed more interesting to examine and since my audience would probably contain more 'lyric' poets than practitioners of other genres, more relevant to them.

I had a pre-existing intention - to write, some time or other, lyrics to this, one of my favourite Monk tunes. The first line came to me in that twilight zone when you emerge from sleep, half-conscious that you are still in dream territory where contours, colours and voices have a pleasant fluidity and autonomy, yet half-aware that you have a composer's role in all of this, that you can snap into full conscious control if you choose.

When I decided to get up, write the line down and keep going, my conscious mind was most concerned with technical problems – negotiating the limits imposed: the number of syllables, the rhythm accents, making sounds that could be assimilated into the octave jumps, the soaring or swooping of the notes and the cross-currents of the tune's momentum.

At the end of the first two lines, however, other unconscious processes were already in play. The first line, the five necessary monosyllables, gave an image which occurs frequently in my work, particularly earlier "juvenile" attempts: the image of looking through glass, sometimes breaking glass, Could this be something of an archetype – the "observer" or commentator torn between a desire to keep apart from the hurly-burly of the world and a desire to be swept up in the stream of existence? I'll leave that for the Freudians and Jungians to debate.

By line two, I had made a decision, unconsciously, to use the first person. It is clear in retrospect that I was already creating an ambivalence – was I identifying with Monk? Was I already embarked on some sort of narrative? Would it be my story or Monk's? Was I trying to get inside his mind or parading my own obsessions?

As the process continued, it was like a river at the tidal limit fed by different tributaries: streams of thought and image which operated, not quite independently, but never fully conscious of a need for, or even a possibility of, integration into a coherent whole. Such is my strong impulse towards narrative and logical structure, that, despite myself, as the poem developed, a ghost of a narrative line began to appear and the images arranged themselves into an almost coherent pattern. This was only clear after the poem was finished. (There was no editing and no second draft.)

The elements of coherence come from the sketchy details I knew about Monk: the possible existence of mental illness, long periods of social and musical isolation, an obsession with his craft and a stubborn refusal to compromise, dependence on the women in his life not just for support, but given his fragile mental state, for mere survival.

The ghost-structure goes something like this: Monk is at a window looking down far into the street; he feels a detachment from self, a not unfamiliar symptom of some mental disorders; he may be waiting for a session with a therapist; he feels a sinister impulse…jump? The images come largely from his absorption with music; he thinks of his wife and dedicates the tune to her, mixed with messages of gratitude and appeals for help. But, importantly, all of this perceived structure was seen only in retrospect. There was no conscious attempt to tell a story. There was another "tributary". In my identification with Monk, a part of my brain was focussed on the my own "story". My wife had recently had a birthday and I had, as I often do, tried to write her a little personal poem, expressing some of the feelings I had been attributing to Monk.

I don't want to suggest the operation here of anything unearthly and mystical. Perhaps if you work in genres which engage with the compositional processes of non-verbal communication (music, mime, visual arts) you are more likely to have a sense of being less fully in conscious "control", Perhaps if you are by inclination a teller of stories, you shouldn't attempt lyric – your instincts will betray you every time. Perhaps this is simply a description of pre-composition, a pre-draft which should be decently buried when the beautiful finished creature has emerged from the chrysalis. Certainly I make no extravagant claims for the quality of the result, a copy of which I have included with this little essay. At least my old friend, the ex-muso thinks it is a brave attempt to perform the impossible. In his words: *Monk! Jesus! You couldn't even scat one of those bastards!*

John Carey

Monk's Mood
(for Christine)

Breath fogs up the glass.
Where is it coming from but me?
Whispers as noiseless as sand
spilling through the waist of an hourglass.
Cars carve up the street
a dozen floors below
moving in grooves like the coloured slabs
of switches in the mixing-room.
Whose are these fingers spread
like soft black spiders in a mating dance?
Who made the space in my head
taking out one sense at a time?
First I'm diving-deaf
then blind, leaning on a touch of your hand
then dumb, swimming in the calm of your eyes,
then blank as an empty waiting room.
Take these notes I string,
A necklace to kiss your throat
made out of silver hammers
and whizzing pinballs from the cup of my brain.
Wear it like a blessing
from someone you loved and lost too soon
and warm me in your heart,
make me the page you never want to turn
make yours the flesh that pins me to the earth.

John Carey

Olga

Is there anything less than Passion
behind your vibrating eyelashes?

Your hands
your words
an extension of dreaming…
a naïvety of general perception…
an instant convalescence of wounded lives…

Your faith in all the revelations
that others designated,
long before you,
for a universal dismissal…

The word *disappointment*'s
withdrawn from your dictionary
with a stroke of joy
and trust…
and even an exhausted muzzle
of a yawning moon
that wades through maimed branches
of dying trees
delivers waltzing meanings.

Who will hurt you, Olga?

In what room,
in which hotel
will you find out
that the walls are painted by
a drunken tradesman
not by *Raphael*?

In the middle of which meadow,

out of a thousand lavish meadows,
will you be looking for
tears you've lost
between daisies and knapweeds?

Who will hurt you, Olga,
by giving you
what you are longing for,
by telling you that there is
an indefinable quantity of
springs,
roads
and fairytales,
by confining your reality
to acceptable proportions…?

Who will hurt you, Olga?

Bogdan Koca

If there's gold in me
it flows from God
...amen.

If not and I am
perchance toejam
or phlegm in Thy throat
...ahhemmm.

Christopher Bodame

Not a Fairy Tale

He invited me to turn him into a prince
but warts do not invite kisses.
Still, he was the stranger within my gates,
perhaps I should offer him a refuge:
prisms of water trembling on leaves,
a hammock of green,
the cliff-face, a walled turret,
a lookout tower in the camphor laurel.

Uncertain, I played for time,
made a dungeon out of an empty garbage bin
while I contemplated his future
and the commandment *Thou shalt not kill.*
Every day I play with the delicate balance of nature:
dispatch moths, ants, cockroaches,
banish spiders to the garden.
But this was no ordinary interloper;
he should have stayed at home,
not stowed away in a potted palm.

I thought about my guest as I drank tea:
tried to imagine him as a tadpole
swimming in a jar of water from the creek
then the metamorphosis,
and phoned the Museum.
"I've caught a cane toad. Would you like it?"
"No thanks. We've got plenty already."
"What do I do with it?"
"Put it in the freezer till it's dead."

I remember Napoleon:
the retreat from Moscow -
bodies of foot soldiers buried in snow,
and returned to the garden,

peeped in the bin;
the prisoner looked at me, bright-eyed, expectant.
I retreated, a general without an army -
no minions to carry out the death sentence;
vacillated till morning.

At the prison, a trail of ants;
inside, the victim sucked dry,
as flat as a bookmark.
Ignoble death! Poor Toad,
you should have been like you namesake
and stayed inside the page of a book.

Hilarie Lindsay

"Fred has a face you can't remember
even while you are looking at it."

Richard Deutch, after Whiteley

An old man dies
and the mourning in his eyes stare wide
towards the star gleaming skies of his dreaming.
And his stagnant death
goes streaming
into fragrant breath
like fire from deadwood.

Christopher Bodame

Their Place

Oblivion has no stations
on this road.
The hand that touched
the passers-by
many generations ago
again touches them now
and their dust subsides
under their feet
once more.

They had wished
for a knight to come
and he did, passing
quickly, leaving a breeze
that rippled their shirts.

Something fell
from his shadow on the road
and since then
the pedestrians circle
around their place
on the sidewalk
and those who sit
are nailed to their chairs.

Wadih Sa'adeh
Translated from the Arabic by *Sargon Boulus*

Drought

The mortised
red gum posts of the derelict

stockyard have been threaded
with blackberry.

Thistles floss the evening light
across the ridge.

As you poke about the ruins
of the barn, picking

over traces and the other bits
of harness crumbled

into dust, and all
those rusted lumps of cast iron

meaning something
else, once upon a time, realise

this country's foreshortened
history, so much

crowded up against the last two
centuries, so recent

that it's still almost the first day.
Walk on down the road.

Three cows press out the mush
beneath their hooves

in the mud-mascara
about the dam's squinting eye—

as they startle back
it's as if God has grabbed them.

John Allison

Harvest

Tin roof sags,
walls full of holes:
the first snow
or a good hailstorm
will flatten it.

The barn's been empty
since the old cow
was struck by lightning
under the big gum tree
where she's buried.

This summer
she sent up a good crop of daisies.

Hilarie Lindsay

"We came to the city because we heard the country was at war."

Howard Roslington who heard it from his father who heard it from music-hall or the like.

Christmas Bells

I didn't want to come to the city -
to leave country roads and villages, the smell
of dust and eucalypt, stories of the bullock dray
and Evan's ram. Jokes about Gwen's scones.
Life lived in rhythms, drumming rain,
horses in the yards.

That last weekend we camped in the bush,
skin fresh in the morning cold, the waterfall
a shimmer of prismed light.
Blanfordias on hinged stems,
red and orange bells sang out the day
and we danced the slow dance of leaving.

There is the grief of no tears.
Cramped and shut away,
I unpack and negotiate the dark mesh of signs
to strange streets. So much injured land
cast in concrete, frozen away from seasons.

In the shopping centre,
boutiques cram goods into rented holes. The florist
strings a perpetual crowd of bulbs
with turned up collars, sad prisoners
alongside hunched up ferns.
I stop, caught by red gold
flowers confined in too little water
dying, not yet dead, renamed Christmas Bells
in keeping with the season:
life preserved for artless decoration.

Synthesised music tracks, sticky fingers
through myriad zones of pick me up.
Shoppers snap the plastic down,
take up their bags
and walk.
I kneel beside the pail of flowers
weep the bucket full.

Jorie Manefield Ryan

The Schemer

You came zoom-booming into my life
then tip-toed out, back to your wife:
just a gin-sipping,
woman-whipping
man
who can,
only sometimes.

We dreamt of green fields
and love in houses with chimneys
while we were citied, high-rised,
you do-you-like-buttercupping me up with dreams
(and the answer, the answer was yes, more fool I)
watching the shades on my throat change,
never bothering to ask me why
just scheming your schemes.

Sue Hicks

The Shed

I'm married to a bloke with a shed
where we keep the car.
Coming in late I trip over
feral rakes,
traps of rusty wire,
stumble through an ambush
of empty cartons,
old tent poles,
a discarded basketball ring,
bang my head on a bag of old cricket balls
hanging from the rafters
beside the obsolete golf clubs.

I stretch for the light switch,
reach shelves overflowing
with awls, hammers, saws,
chisels, screwdrivers, axes,
a shoe-last,
jam jars full of nails, bolts, screws
and keys that have mislaid their doors.

In the dark recesses under the house
where water seeps through stone
like the cellar of a Scottish laird,
cobweb-covered bottles lie on their sides.

As I reach the sanctuary of my kitchen
I remember my mother's words:
If you want to get married
never beat a man at sport or cards
and wonder
why she never warned me about the shed.

Hilarie Lindsay

Now

Once,
I just had to know
all the ways
things are fucked.

Absolution perhaps:
regret as step one to remission.

I was young:
it was grist for importance.
I played da-da dumb on my drum.

Now, I can no longer bear it:
the frailty
of the few things not fear…

Bad enough beauty evaporates…
but that dreams are engorgements;
whole lives, cul-de-sacs of the prance…

I may not know how this will finish,
but plot is self-interest.

Switch off the justifications.
Let me turn from the story's sad cogs
to the coast of the moment,
watch light bud and flower.

Martin Langford

Thunderstorm after a Drought

The sky at last turns threatening,
billowing, black and menacing.
The birds have fled into the trees
and thunder rolls in far-off flashes,
getting nearer.

Schoolboys pause in their game of football
as the first drops
seem so strange and unfamiliar.
Then comes the torrent, and whooping sounds
as boys shuck shoes and run amok,
as if they had never seen rain before.
Leaves accumulate in drains, the overflow floods,
and the game degenerates into mud
and laughter.

Later, in the cold swish of evening,
I count the pairs of empty football boots
scattered in the empty park, their owners
swept away in the dissolving rain.

John Weerden

the fascination of what's simple

wind   skittering on the surface of water
clouds rippled mares' tales in the sky
ravellingunravelling   white-on-blue
wind-in-the-grass   stayingoingstaying

still things moving   as if   against the sky
the power stanchion forever falling across clouds
kneeling with my ear against cold silvered steel
i was five   listening to its buzzing power

the turning/standing landscape motion outside the train
and the way the horizon rises and falls behind things
as i ride in cars   my childhood horizon   there
mt banks   mt tomah   mt wilson   jellore

walking into/standing against buffeting wind
or on clouded in-house days   hearing it fluting
morning mist   still-floating   above paddocks
rain-scented air   toast on winter mornings

sniffing my fingers for the crush of eucalyptus leaf
chopping hardwood   the smell of it on my hands
smoke   backlit   standing beams in afternoon trees
the stone i drop   plomp   through my reflection

rain applauding corrugated iron and spattering windows
thunderstorm   moving   a rainbow   close-lit golden hills
and   later   night lightning   in the distance   total silence

Bill Tibben

A bird from the East is in town.
It is alive because it is singing.

Shawki Moslemani
Translated from the Arabic **Papers of Solitude**
by *Raghid Nahhas* and *Noel Abdulahad*

The Ten Complicities
(after a Hebrew poem)

They came to take the old growth forests and
I didn't say anything.
They imprisoned the boat people and
I didn't say anything.
They said the parents threw the children overboard and
I didn't say anything.
They said there were weapons of mass destruction and
I didn't say anything.
They said they were going to sell off Telstra and
I didn't say anything.
They deprived indigenous people of a voice, closed down their
legal centres, and I didn't say anything.
They funded the wealthy schools before schools for all and
I didn't say anything.
They want to make our workplaces unsafe with deregulation and
I didn't say anything.
They bought the people with bribes and false promises and
I didn't say anything.
They came to take me away, and I didn't say anything because
I had lost the power of speech.

Margaret Smith

dreams' coral

"In dreams begins responsibility."
epigraph from 'old play' quoted by *W.B. Yeats*
in 'Responsibilities'

"The task of imagination is to imagine the real."
William Lynch

Genesis

With what meagre space
remaining between his hands
he tried to reconstruct
a universe: with a tear,
he drew a star, a moon with a glance,
and with a single touch, a sun.

When he closed his eyes,
people commuted to their work
on the sidewalk of his eyelids.

Wadih Sa'adeh
Translated from the Arabic by *Sargon Boulus*

Leonardo's Horses

All those sketches
to understand what makes a horse.
Muscles, sinews, the power
of moving legs and joints tethered to the page.
Thousands of hair-thin strokes
drawn searching for its soul.

The secrets of Bucephalus
hidden in the swish of tail, a twitch of skin
as he runs a hand over a foreleg
for the shape of bone.

Drawing the rein along its neck,
he slips his leg across its back,
lies along its length
to feel the body heat and breath.

Huddles over the neck, lets the horse take off
and leap into a gallop on the pasture's slope,
surging and jerking with every stride;
a blur across the landscape.

Leonardo wiping wind-tears from his eyes.
The stallion striding home
as if it owns the whole green earth.

Paula McKay

Making Room

We have found a home, after terrible wanderings
together. Once, in Rome,
we were trapped. You were delirious
with fever, there was no money for food,
and I watched you in terror, thinking
this is the end. Suddenly
you woke, and said, "I've been thinking.
When all this is over
we might have a daughter. I'd like that."
But I couldn't answer, afraid to look
beyond the room at the shimmering
heat outside.

This morning, our kitten sleeps
on my lap, white limbs spread delicately
as anemones. At night she creeps
amongst my hair and nuzzles, dimly
seeking milk in the darkness. Her purring
vibrates through my head
till each strand becomes
awake and electric. Now, I remember my dream
of a girl who is our daughter.
She turns to me smiling, and points
through the window. I look, and see
the ocean dreaming itself
deep blue
and the evening sky and the swans
that seem to cover the world as we watch them,
lost in the spell
of their quietness.

Love, we have made room
here for a kitten who flies through the house
ringing bells and flashing teeth
and claws. We have struggled
to this small space,
scarcely able to know
how we've survived.

Now,
when I'm frightened, I remember the day
how starving and ill
you still hoped to provide,
and saw through the window
the image
of our child.

Yvonne Deutch

A cat tinkles discord on a piano
missing two teeth.
A child peers out between the shutters.

Upon your face, subliminal light
reflections.
Starglints.

Robert Balas

Mood Lighting

I had the tradesmen come in
to change the lounge and sitting rooms.
New lighting, I wanted more light.
21 halogen lights with dimmer switches,
and a lighter colour on the walls.

Luff it was called,
and new ceilings,
to be white and flat and smooth,
yes smooth, without a mark or scratch,
no champagne cork marks,

no rubber ring marks from toy guns,
and the floors sanded, then polished,
cut back to remove the scuff marks
of the departed kids
and the dog who died last month.

The rooms are all inner city minimalist,
just a little furniture.
Friends come to dinner,
"You have mood lighting!"
they say admiringly.

John Weerden

They said
grass has dried on the souls of your children...
and birds died inside the cages of their eyes.

A child's hand
is a brush
painting a bird
in space.

Shawki Moslemani
Translated from the Arabic **Papers of Solitude**
by *Raghid Nahhas* and *Noel Abdulahad*

O earth, fire, wind, water:
play your alchemy.
Ancient mysteries live on in a simple loaf;
life laid down, fire transfigured:
dough becomes bread.

O earth, fire, wind, water:
play, transfigure me.
Starting at shadows I lose my way;
help me be, be still
touching into light.

Neil Anderson

The Light Continent

The child unwrapped
from the leaves of sleep,
shuttled dream-eyed
to a gleam of dark water.

What mother I to
trust such precious cargo
to a craft makeshift
in sea-worth and guile.

Magic mantras I know
to muzzle sea monsters,
rein monsoons,
tame the tempest,
disarm distances.

Secret chambers
bear wombfruit to fullness.

Mama, is there such a thing as black light?
Mama, the sky has no corners!
Mama, if we have no money, can we buy some?
Mama, does God have a God?
Mama, the bathtub is filled to the brim!

O save, not savage.
Gratitude not graves.
Wombfruit not wormfood.
Morning not mourning.

Odyssey, half blind,
to the light continent.
Behind, the broken,

the golden chersonese.

When I was a child
I swam in jade seas
careless of jellyfish.

Don't stop the city
but give me a space
in which I can, my beloved
hold, behold, be whole.
Can I, my beloved,
love, be loved, be lovely?

Live, believe.
Live, betray.
Love, be true.

Child in snow mountains, swollen
and shoeless in a new world order.

Sweet brow, breath, cheek:
dear heart, being.
Profoundly child,
as if have need to be any else
(but) child incarnate,
rose of the cosmos.

Ten Ch'in Ü

"Everything hinges upon whether you believe in infinity."
Charles Plumridge

Attempt to Connect Two Shores with Sound

You wanted something flying. You requested tobacco and added siblings to the doves in the empty space of the room. You wanted something flying, something coming out of the window, so you threw yourself through the glass. But a spot of blood which came out of you stayed on the inside.

You are the one who now is in another place, and three ducks sleep in front of your house; you who would stare at the walls in order to hear the voices of your parents commenting. Let me speak to you, then: listen to my voice, my voice from this place which is your voice from the other place.

The hour they knew, some of them wailed in mourning and some of them remained silent as they accompanied us to our final place. They took us in a box, borne on eight hands and many glances. You were looking at me, the one living in you, as I looked at you, the dead one in me. You wanted to smile at me, and I wanted to bewail you, but we were silent and we left them to bury us there.

We are the two speaking to themselves now, you from there, and I from here, the one we: the living speaking with his dead self; what have we hereafter besides memory?

Our family doesn't have ducks; except that, from the frequency with which we dreamt of them, they finally came and slept on our door.

But you were leaving.

They arrived and saw no blood. The blood stayed on the inside. It wasn't on the inside completely, nor on the outside completely. On the edge of them both. On the glass. On the edge which was neither on the outside nor on the inside.

You're the one sleeping now, and you are not concerned with blood. The one sleeping far-off, while three ducks sleep in front of your house. Don't worry - I will feed them. There is grain in the cupboard, which you purchased one evening, when you were walking alone in the city dreaming of them.

And they've come.

But they, too, haven't seen your blood.

Other creatures also came. People and trees and birds; and they didn't see your blood. They escorted you to your grave and came back.

They carried you because you were unable to reach there yourself.

They rained dirt on you so you would disappear.

Between these walls you spent your life. You were born in the corner, and the furthest journey was from wall to wall.

You wanted something else. Your scream was nothing but a call to this thing outside, so you could get out, even if only one drop of blood got out the window.

Since your birth you have been invoking nothing but death.

Give me a glass of water. Thirsty, I want to drink. Just give me some indication that you still see me.

Your eyes are closed, there's dirt on them. Your eyes are empty.

You see me with two emptinesses, and hear me with two emptinesses. Your emptiness is my full listener and seer. Neither sound nor light passes through what is full. Hear me then and look at me.

Death? We knew then: outside - that's death.

Where are the angels? Tell the angels to come - here, we've arrived. We don't want a death with no angels. We have ashes with which to entertain ourselves for all eternity. An angel's wing flutters and scattered particles fly, the spirits of doves fly, siblings of doves which were in that room. An angel alights and we feed it whispers, we feed it glances and entertain ourselves. So let the angels come; we have arrived.

We have ashes, we'll entertain ourselves for all eternity

We've arrived...but the angels too were dead!

Forty-eight years - this was the time, then.

This was the bottleneck of eternity, which we thought was a long embrace, the mouth we kissed under a quick-moving cloud.

When we were born, rain poured down from our mother's skin. Rain stayed in the corner near the threshold - it too stayed inside. Those outside didn't see it, nor did those who came in. It was a rain peculiar to her alone, watering her interior field which no one sees.

And when we were leaving, a rain came pouring down too. On the people, on the wood and trees, on stone...but it was a rain very far, far-off.

It came pouring down there, far away in the place which they call life.

This is time, then. This is eternity: forty-eight years!

And before that nothing, and after that nothing.

Here we are, two nothingnesses talking, two emptinesses trying to fill up with sound.

Join your voice to mine; join your silence to my silence. Perhaps they will become a voice.

Nothingness is what we are now. That's us, nothing else.

Talk to me about your first sound, your first game, about the tiny arm around your mother's neck, about your shoes in the fields. Speak, make sounds: fill this nothingness.

Our mother says our first sound was a scream. She tossed the burden of firewood from her back before the oven door and minutes later she heard the first of our sounds, our voices.

Those around her said "Congratulations!" Their speech reached her from among her body's drizzle, like a rainbow she would see in winter.

We were born in July, at the height of summer, and yet it was raining!

But is was a rain peculiar to her alone, promising her flowers and fruit...as for us, we were crying!

At that time I gave you my first look, as someone looks at morning in a mirror and walks away.

I have nothing to say. I just want to talk, to make a bridge of sounds to bring me to myself. Two far-off shores I am trying to join by sound.

The words are sounds, sounds, nothing else. So it is now, so it always was. Sounds we direct at no one. We are not bespeaking others. We are just talking to ourselves. Others are a strange and far-off thing which we don't see or know, and practically, they don't exist.

Speech is nothing but isolation, nothing but silence.

Nonetheless I want to talk now; I want to repeat my isolation.

But what does one who is dead say to himself?

They're both here now - Memory which closed the door behind it and Forgetfulness standing at the threshold. Here they're hovering around the figment of a spirit. The spirit fell from the window and its figment came to meet it as far as the door. And I write in order to remember the body of this spirit, in order to remember that I had a body. That there was body hair on my body and I don't know what happened to it. In order to remember more precisely that what I had was body hair, not a body; and that I did nothing all my days but search for my body.

Sometimes I would be pervaded by the feeling that humankind lives with no body. They keep on in life as long as they are searching for their bodies, and when they give up the search, they die.

I myself lived with no body. I was overflowing with spirit but I was with no body. My spirit looked for my body at length. It went limping, lost, mad. And it remained alone, it remained floating particles, a desiccated spirit searching for a drop and when it cast itself from the window only a drop of blood was to be seen. Blood, they said, is to run in bodies! But the drop of blood remained up on the edge, between the inside and outside, on the borders which don't belong to anyone.

I wanted something to fly, something to come out of the window.

I had no body. But something strange was stuck to me.

Was that strange thing my body?

So let's laugh, let's open our two mandibles and laugh. Your laugh coming forth from two empty bones will be more beautiful than what is in this text, believe me.

You are the hero of this text, even if you are a dead hero. But when I want you alive, you must live. Writers move their characters as they wish and you must move as I want, even if you are dead. Don't say that the bier is narrow and you've become dust. It's up to writers to move the dust and widen biers. They have to bring the dead back to life too.

You were always rebellious. You cut off your life zealously, like one who cuts the branch over his head with a sword.

And we were, you and I, on two fronts. We have to fight ferociously and negotiate submissively. We won't arrive at a peace or a truce.

You are dead before me now, and I want you to admit that you were my enemy, and that our enmity to ourselves was more ferocious than our enmity to others. Others are something else. If you are incapable of killing them, you can just forget them; but how do you forget yourself? One solution is before you: to kill it! And you killed it!

So let's laugh, then, before this victory. Before the hidden drop of blood. And let's remember our body which was wrapped in closed skin.

Our body, our frightening inner darkness! And I remember now how the blood looked running its way in the veins! And how these innards lived for years without seeing anything!

Our body was murdered. Murdered by its blindness. Murdered by the desire to see. Its darkness and its light are its murderers. The darkness and light which both call a knife to open an aperture.

From this aperture I see you now. The aperture which you opened yourself. You couldn't bear your inner darkness. You wanted light for the blood and sight for the innards. You kindled a light for the skin and blood and innards, and for death too.

Our comrades would describe Hope as light. They say

"the light of hope." You, though, chose the light of death.

They came up with adjectives for everything, and they wanted them utterly sweet and having a reverberation. Like one insisting on devising a sound for the footsteps of people who have become absent.

In the beginning there were adjectives, and it was up to us to devise things to apply them to.

It was up to us to create a universe from mere attributes!

We created a universe, and we put life in it. But what we had collected was not life but death. Life was for differentiation. We were reconciled for the first time when we died.

I am not searching now for the light of life. No, but for a warming fire.

In heaven are spirits shivering from cold. I want to kindle a fire for them. I want to button up their shirt buttons.

We possessed a little screaming and with this scream one day we said to life, "We love you".

We went looking for friends, for people, for plants, for stones, to madly extol our love to them. We went in order to tear our heart apart.

We saw places for everything. For ants, for trees, for birds, for the earth, for the stars. Where is the place of our love?

Where do we put this love? Where do we house this animal? Our shoulders have hunched over.

We walked all the streets, all the places, and all of them were full. The earth was full before our arrival, and what we bear came to have no place. We became the one place for our burden. We became the illusion of its place. Its place is our illusion and our place is its illusion. It and we and the place became an illusion.

In the beginning was the illusion. Illusion became an earth on which we came down.

The illusion of earth gave birth to the illusion of desire. And the illusion of desire gave birth to the illusion of love. And the illusion of love gave birth to the illusion of birth.

And the illusion of birth gave birth to the illusion of life. And the illusion of life gave birth to the illusion of forgetfulness. And the illusion of forgetfulness gave birth to isolation...

From the illusion of earth to the illusion of love is fourteen illusions. And from the illusion of love to the illusion of life is fourteen illusions. And from the illusion of life to isolation is fourteen illusions...

In the beginning was the illusion. And illusion became body and came down among us.

Ah Monique, O one giving illusions a beautiful body. You were sleeping on the ground so let it not be said that you rose one cubit towards the illusions, but rather that you were sleeping there so they could descend unto you.

And they descended. They washed your eyes, your mouth, your neck, your chest, your pubes, your legs, so you could go to sleep clean.

O Monique who was sleeping on the ground, where are you now? I am two metres underground, and under my bones is a stone bothering me. Tell someone to knock away this stone, I want to sleep.

We walked a lot, searching for a little love. We walked with short statures on long roads, and we were almost to be seen.

“We want love,” we screamed. Love lengthens our stature.

Dalal gave us her sacred lock, Hoda the key of her gate, Ghada her bolt, and Auror children.

O mistress of the sacred lock, O guardian of the gate, O lady of the bolt, O mother of children, we want love, we want a place.

So let the water rise so the deluge surges, so alarm overwhelms the high rivers. I want a little water. Just so that these fish in my bowl don’t die.

I am dead enough, and I have time to weave dreams. Dead enough to devise the life I wanted.

It isn’t beautiful, Wadi’, to lie down for all eternity without dreaming. It isn’t beautiful, in death too, to not live the life which you have longed for.

Death is wide, broad enough for everything. Forget the narrow planet earth. Sway in your wide void, in your nothingness, and laugh long.

Nothingness is wide open, you can protract your laugh in it forever.

Wadih Sa’adeh
Translated from the Arabic by *Clarissa C. Burt*

Why I Write

Let's start down the track that leads to vanity publishing:
my own satisfaction, set down my thoughts, crystallise ideas,
embed an experience in the page, have it on tap for recall.
Leave a record for friends and family of who I was.
Why poetry? It's shorter. It's multi-faceted. It's truer.
You can find the minutiae in parish registers and family albums.
Or take the Narcissus track to the ornamental lake,
make interesting noises for your own delectation
or the ennoblement of some putative posterity –
a monument more lasting than bronze. Or disclaim
all responsibility – the Devil makes me or the Muse
or a sputtering fuse of genetic coding. Or take the Sociological
Track – I was no good at football, it was all I could do
to earn some grudging respect from my peers. Or be a full-
blown Andersonian – what's partly true is completely a lie.
I simply don't know. It's like being asked by a friend
your opinion of marriage. What can you say? When I was single,
I liked being single. Now I'm married, I like being married.
When I didn't write, I was mostly happy with that.
Now I write a lot, I wouldn't want it any different.
Or take the communication path. We are social animals.
I write to somebody, for somebody. If I didn't write, there'd
be no point to it. What I write and how I write is determined
in large part by this as well as by the limits of what
I'm good enough to write. I'm not primarily writing
for publishers and editors of Academic Journals, not because
it's an unworthy thing, but because I think that for me
it's an unrealistic target. I'm writing for my peers-
people not much unlike myself, unsurprisingly.
Of a certain age and background, probably, well-educated,
probably, but not hard-core intellectuals. People who go
to poetry readings and like to respond to something
at a single hearing, and just maybe, pick up a copy and read it
sometime with some pleasure in the recall and maybe even

a bit of subtext that missed their attention or listen to
the spaces if I had the skill or luck to suggest the existence
of spaces…as if! …you wish! …fat chance!
Yes, of course, this isn't the whole story. You want to make
something beautiful, however strange and elusive and hard
to define. We humans are pattern makers, obsessive weavers
of meaning. Something in us abhors chaos and letting go,
drives us to the edge of abyss or maelstrom, tempts us
to throw ourselves into the midst, yet makes us shrink
away from it, clutch at the lifebuoy of meaning or religion
or race-memory or ego, anything that defies the flux
of incoherence that keeps winking at us from the porch,
inviting us to nothingness or Hell.

John Carey

Everybody's a Critic

It was Washington University St Louis where presidental candidates seem to also get into altercations. In my case I was leaving a party when a total and totally drunk stranger tackled me from the back. I rolled over, started warding off his punches karate style, fists closed at my wrists. I doubt if the next morning he could have told you why he did this maybe even *that* he did it. We didn't know one another. The guys were pulling him off me and girls looking over their shoulders when I heard one guy say, "We've got to protect our poets." A pause. Then he added, "Even the bad ones."

Richard Deutch

Night Fishing off Don Bank

We ply our lines
hoping to make hooks in the air,
we set our lures, brightly coloured,
dressed in our attempt at alchemy,
for immortality's granite form, to budge one iota.
We are as hopeful as the salmon
confronting the sheer cliff of spawn's necessity,
        to see our creations
sparkling on the dinner plates of the successful,
forsaking the unbecoming, inky depths,
where dreams' coral, of impossible beauty, lies
        unlighted:
they gave us their lives to escape.

Danny Gardner

Sigh 1

If one was adept only
At tracing a given shape
Or at reshaping all that's been given
Without the aiding and abetting
Of the rules of perception,

One would not necessitate
One's own subsistence

Bogdan Koca

"Stop thinking, start dreaming." *Tao-Li*

This Side

"I see black light."
    Victor Hugo

"It's getting dark."
He told me this towards the end when he'd gone
beyond the mountain hut where scientists
were working at their apparatus—
such things my father saw, looking from the bed
through that open window only he could see.

"That waterfall, now where d'you reckon
that might be, eh chum?"
He'd discovered one, years before
on a survey expedition up the back of Torrent Bay.
But towards the end he went
beyond the mountains he loved, turning
down the morphine so he wouldn't be mistaken.

Each night I tried to look out through that window.
In the frame myself, the polished sheen
of a black mirror always looking back at me.
Yes, there is another way of looking:
darkness is not absence but more intimate a presence—
silence, and the sound of it,
and mountains, rivers, waterfalls,
that sudden evening rise of rainbow trout.

John Allison

Motherland

My first memories are clear, if a trifle exaggerated. I was born, I am told, on the back of a giant jellyfish. It had become encrusted with the things of the sea throughout the ages in which it had floated on the waves, following its purposes; it was hard and knobbly, carvable in places, sprinkled with small land and marine plants and harmless growths, not an uncongenial surface upon which to make a home. From the few fragile shrubs on the crown and the irregular projections of our home hung folded fruit bats. Below the surface of the sea loomed its atrocious underbelly, transparent and glutinous, releasing noxious belches with each contraction of its bell which left a cloudy residue in the sea all around. This usually subsided to a welcome lull at sundown, making it safe to leave the creature carefully by means of a small boat, and even paddle in the waters out of reach of the tentacles. Then, on summer evenings, as the moths that made their home on the jellyfish stirred and choked the warm air, we could watch dolphins frolic in the dimming light and even join their sport, clutching their fins as they sped across the water or throwing up objects for them to catch. They were closest to humans of all the creatures I knew, closer even than the gnarled tortoises with their ridiculous gait and absence of mind. Their spirit was light-hearted, a created variant of our sobriety. They would go south in the winter and northwards in the spring, and although not we but our jellyfish decided on our course as we had no way of steering it, our paths would always meet, as if even the jellyfish followed a navigational pattern - one, perhaps, of deliberate irregularity. Its mind was unknown, not like that of other living things.

My father was an inventor. He had fashioned our home according to the curves of the jellyfish's armoured back out of debris fished from the sea. The front door was a haphazard wing of mother-of-pearl; the stairway, the inner spiral of an outsize shell. My father worked every day in a large library filled with light, planning new domes and towers and decorative ingenuities, continually changing the appearance of our home, extending it and embellishing the extensions. A device to predict the weather, attached to a wand at the top of the house, hung in the centre of the kitchen which was round and had a floor of red earth. There were tunnels too, underground chambers and streams in which rainwater collected and where I was always afraid to go in case I met a tortoise in the dark or even something malign; I knew that after rain, improbable creatures would appear from under stones - an armoured beast that walked on its fleshy elephantine nostrils, lizards that spat streams of blood from their eyes, tiny undulating worms which could spring to the height of a grown man or stinking carnivorous beetles - I in my forgotten state did not think to question their existence.

My mother was a siren. Her voice would echo through the great cavities of the jellyfish producing harmonics and overtones; rushing through the tunnels, it would split at the forks and emerge at each end as a different note, one high and one low. She could imitate the voices of birds and the calls of whales, remember thousands of sailors' songs from a time before that of the floating jellyfish, incant lines of ancestral poetry, or create arabesque translations of my father's wild spires. Her voice would awaken me at sunrise with its tragic purity, and thrum me to sleep in the twilight, accompanied by the lapping of the waves and the occasional stirring of the jellyfish's tentacles. Alone of her kind, my mother was often to be found looking far out to sea with her hair dripping, a look of passion on her face, in a kind of silent deadlock. At these times, she would cast and recast her oracle bones. Her song, although ever immaculate and captivating, had long since been nullified of its danger. I don't remember ever being afraid that she would leave, although I have often since asked myself if she was content.

I remember sitting up far into the night watching the gradual opening of a great white flower of intoxicating perfume that blooms once a year as sprays of light could be seen high in the sky quite a distance away. I was told that these were fireworks. They occurred night after night and we stayed out on the verandah, the intact cartilage fin of a sea monster, watching them while surrounded by the whizzing and plopping of flying fish. We took it in turns to read from books of poetry - my mother combing her hair with a five-pronged shell and my father blowing smoke-rings from a long pipe while sharpening his carving tools - until the sailors sending them up grew tired of the display. It was a token, this peculiarly human festivity, from the world beyond and although it made me hotly curious I made no move to explore it (which was in any case impossible).

On another occasion as the jellyfish drew into strange tropical waters, a population of large colourful birds of diverse species descended upon it, taking possession of the trees and filling the air with ceaseless chatter and screaming quarrels. Their dung covered the ground in a thick sticky layer, making it impossible to walk on and attracting insects in their thousands. My parents cursed the birds but I was intrigued by them and grew admirous of their various calls, a ringing net of exuberant sound that would begin before dawn, and when the jellyfish meandered on towards colder regions I was disappointed to see them fly away in a great swirling column taking their young, now fully grown, with them. It was then that I discovered that no state on the jellyfish's back was ever permanent.

(fragment)

Miranda Su Lan Harding

Note on 'grew admirous'

"*Growing admirous* is a state of being, an entity full of admiration. I miss this active quality in the less extravagant 'admire' which has a much more distanced and less intuitive relationship with the object of admiration."

Miranda Su Lan Harding

letter while flying

"Your innermost happening is worth all your love."

Rainer Maria Rilke

'Letters to a Young Poet'

The Greenshank
for Juno

In a trench, Miklos Radnoti
noticed it was spring, petals of crushed flowers
floated in a wake of scent.
His lover's face appeared, he caressed her neck,
then wrote a sonnet in his notebook -
lead flying, he scrawled words
with the stub of his pencil.

Just after dawn today, the news echoed lies.
Radnoti's love poem was wiped away
with wings and petals. Hungarian fascists
following their orders.

The full light, outside the windows,
your unbending will -
our sanctuary, Mondrian's concepts
made of glass and cedar, this river chapel house.

This afternoon just before dark
the first greenshank from the Hebrides arrived.

Migrating across human borders
landing on the mudbank.
Its technology feathers and fish-fuel, cryptic colours.

This elegant wader from Scotland's lowlands
ruffled in the westerly, took off again
and with an acrobatic twist skimmed over a hummock.

Its beak conducted the rising and falling of its song.
This lone greenshank dashed across mudflats
stood on one leg, then came forward in a high stepping dance.

Robert Adamson

A Wanting Experience
(To my friend Anis)

I believe that poetry is a salvation piece of wood onto which a drowning person of a different kind clings to, despite knowing that it will not save him from sinking. And I trust that life is a tumbling boat but we can always move into other vessels where new life exists. I also suppose that the human being is the trustee of this life regardless of the many obstacles he or she faces and despite being deeply submerged in barbarism.

That is why I scream out in pain in my poetry more than I happily cry. And this is also why I always open a window in my poetry. I know that my private tunnel is dark and closed, but I do realize, too, that the tunnels of others will one day be brighter than mine.

With this background I write poetry. And perhaps because of this, most of my verses are short. Is it because I know that deliverance by a piece of timber is illusionary indeed? Or is this because I should hold on to something, although imaginary, so I may proceed in life?

(fragment)

Shawki Moslemani
Translated from the Arabic by *Anton Sabella*

Whole Life Plus Profits

Fill up the form says the insurance man,
Do fill it up,
There's a good chap.
Answer the questions as best you can.

All right, I say, that's not my age,
I had a proposal declined
And nearly went out of my mind.
That's all I'm prepared to tell you at this stage.

I do get dizzy, sometimes I forget.
This anxious cloud at the top is my head.
Some mornings I can't get out of bed
And that down there is a spigot, not a threat.

Strange to be owner at last of all this fear.
I was out for cover, no less,
Not for death but nakedness.
I can't read forms, I've put the wrong name here.

John Miles

Reality Number Six

Matthew:

I am glad...yes I'm glad that you have been able to withdraw yourself from...you see, I have to talk to somebody...I want to talk to you...and I want to tell you something, which is so intimate and so bizarre that...I can't actually talk about it to anyone who listens...who hears, you see. Not because it is a secret, no, it is nothing of the sort, but I'm ashamed of myself...of my thoughts of...well...of my being. On the other hand I want to believe that somebody listens to me...I need to believe this. It is up to me of course...and now I have the chance...I can pretend that you are listening...you are present after all. You are here. You are completely dead, so to speak, but I don't have to know it...so I'll pretend that you are my interlocutor who listens in silence and then I will ask you at the end: "What do you think about it Lawrence?" and then it'll become obvious to me that all my effort was absolutely worthless. No it won't do. I have to come up with a better conclusion...we will see...Dear Lawrence, I am not what I really am...I am an intellectual zero, nothing...I am a writer who doesn't know what he is writing...I have no concepts, no ideas, no talent, no nothing...I am completely empty, worthless, I am, in fact nobody...I read about my so called great ideas, great novels and plays...they write about me, they analyse me, they praise me, they learn from me, they tell things about me that I can't understand... all my life was like that...I never understood a single word I wrote... I don't know what I am writing about or...It has just happened to me. Accidentally. I wrote, as a joke, three pages, it was long before you were born, Lawrence...and then somebody, who was insane, but well connected, read it. Accidentally. He asked me what I was trying to say and I replied, just out of the blue: "What

I really mean", I said, "is the deepest secret of my very existence, it is the secret of the independent soul of an artist who is at large and will never ever be comprehended for he is like a mercury which changes his own shape and his own matter." He didn't say a word. He hugged me and then he published these 3 pages with 47 pages of his own introduction, which ends with the words: "The Genius was reborn tonight". Then he died next day. Suicide. I told one critic that this man was insane. He replied: "You know, you are the most modest eccentric I have ever met." That's what he said. They called me a philosopher, the father of a new trend and so on...they invented a new name for my literature, they claimed that a new form of artistic expression was born and I was the father of it. *Mercurism*. I am the forefather of *Mercurism*, do you hear? Painters, theatre practitioners, photographers, filmmakers, musicians, even fashion designers...everyone is creating within the frame of *Mercurism*. They can't create in any other fashion because *Mercurism* excludes any possibility of escape. Whatever you do it always will be...it will be forever *Mercurism*...There isn't even the possibility of inventing any other style since *Mercurism* itself is perfectly deprived of any style...They created a theory for it, you know. It is madness...And I am the father of it. I know nothing. I was even trying to write against the rules of grammar, against anything I considered logical, or tangible, or useful...a failure. Whatever I did scribe on a piece of paper would instantly become 'the classic', 'a new archetype', 'an achievement'. I can't cope with this any more, Lawrence. I once said I was a con man...I said it publicly and they published a book entitled "An Oral Aspect of *Mercurism* - Theory and Practice" it was the book of the year. I have never consciously created anything, I am not an artist, I am not even ignorant. They call me the greatest ever communicator of humanity...How could it be if I can't even explain to the world my own misery, my own falsehood? Whatever I say, even something incredibly stupid and trivial is taken as holy wisdom. I am unhappy, Lawrence and I am forced to hide my unhappiness. My unhappiness is my deepest secret and is guarded inside me by...*Mercurism*...(Pause) I want to ask you something, I want you to tell me what you think about it all, but...well, I know it might be a bit embarrassing for you...so, please, take it easy...forget about this conversation...just pretend you haven't heard anything.

(fragment)

Bogdan Koca

Sigh 13

There is a sand-martin
Resting on an electric wire

Against a blue time without end

No song is written or sang

An elfin cloud brushes over its feet

Its frail wings mull over
A pending lot

Bogdan Koca

Manly Ferry

Commuting, often I have risked this crossing
lost in thought, rocked by grey waves. Today, also,
I seek a passage over water. Thick as a python
the mooring rope, wound-up and thrown on deck.
The hidden engine stutters, starts,
the ferry moves away. Ripe faces tucked into turtlenecks,
we squint at the welding of sea and sky.

Jakob Ziguras

Somewhat dangerous

teeter
theatre

for the time being
the human being.

sleep sloth nesting
in the shadows
now stirs
another small tiredness.

Will it topple?
Will it topple?
Asha, five, asks
rocking in the rattan chair for the first time.
No, it won't,
unless you rock very hard and fast.
Oh she says rocking very, very fast and hard.

Ten Ch'in Ü

Something of the Eagle
to Ted Hughes

Among us, that Predator, Fate,
occasionally deposits an alien witness.
Like this man from the North,
master of elemental rhythms,
born as much from nature's rhimy slick,
calves' afterbirth and a maggot's imprint,
as the ragings and caressings
of wind and rain, on silk and stone;
seeded in the trapped jaguar's deadly grace,
or the joy of salmon propelled upward by blind lust.
This Laureate, the poet,
anointed at Her Majesty's request,
talked like a local in a Yorkshire pub,
yet was counselled by the planets.

He could set himself apart,
it seems, from those butterfly nets: tragedy and joy.
He dealt in imperatives before feelings.
His failings were concentrated, classically,
on human affairs.
Two partners died, some say needlessly.
Was his, like Hitler's self-loathing,
drawn magnetically to destruction -
if only to survive it?
Yet, he could be considerate, in peace's name,
and when the child called "Daddy! Daddy! Come see!"
even as emotion shrank from
that part of him the cancer had eaten.

At cloudy death's cleansing trumpet
he saw something of the eagle, perhaps,
reflected in his last mirror:
one eye kindly, one eye cold:
the essential duality.

The better for the psyche to apprehend,
the inevitability of the vulture
swooping on fragile prey
and a world of men, rejecting
the inward-seeing blood-sense, of a mere poet,
as if to leave the queasy solace of religion: self-hypnosis

the only escape between fear and thrall.

Danny Gardner

Dual -Thought

You grace us as we pass,
paddle-feet with orange beak and plumage
smiling white.
Children
stop by the pond
merging with their gaze,
and we too, feel this:
how our doors open on every side
with the moving animals—
dipping ducks,
wings in the wind above,
and memories' extended glances.
Yet
comes the thought
falling
in our heart,
of hands deformed,
of wording mouth turned
beak –
so powerless
we stand before their confinement.

Luke Fischer

Ropes

What is a rope? Some sort of super-string maybe,
The key that may unlock physics' crucial riddle?
Does supple, shifting shape suggest a Buddha nature?
Only some magic trick can resolve such questions.
Ropes either connect or measure separation,
They may be rough or smooth, if only long enough,
Justice they serve by hanging or tying up in knots.
Some people walk on ropes, unleashing trains of thought
Along the trail of Zarathustra's parables –
The stumbling clown who faltered, falling to his death
Before a shining hero bridged the widest gap
To reach the rainbow's end, a superhuman goal
(Perhaps he found Valhalla – the legend doesn't tell).
And in between these two? Ordinary mortals
Will sometimes venture over dark, mist-bound paths
As hazardous and as narrow as a tight-rope
Where both departure and final destination
Have lost their definition, dimmed in dream-like blur.
Their poise endangered, as if dangling in mid-air,
Expected satisfaction receding from their view –
Their past a disillusion, the future unfulfilled.
I know one such: he'd stood within a parting gate
And when he took the plunge across the threshold
He left behind him the peace that stems from heaven
In search of greener pastures – paradise on earth.
It still eludes him: no nearer for his troubles
To a shifting mirage in a barren desert –
Enslaved to Circe or to Morganatic Fey
For the full term of his unnatural life
Sentenced to dwell, between two hells, in limbo.

Rene Manning

The Feather Atonement

I journeyed through Holland in September – the train rolling past flat, juicy meadows, the dykes' water levels reflecting bulky cumulus and sunlight moist with almost transparent autumn cloud.

My hosts took me to a European puppet festival at Meppel. The puppets were made with care and precision. My story begins with a brief recollection of a Flemish play.

A man lay in bed next to his spouse, dreaming he had caught a feather from a visiting angel's wing. The next morning, true to all prophetic dreams, the feather lay lightly upon his pillow. His heart swelled with budding warmth. He turned to his wife, speaking quickly and with unrestrained joy about the night-time vision. "Just an old feather," she said. "Must have found its way out of our eiderdown."

Later on that day, walking to the park, he showed it to a child. Surely a child would know about angels' wings? The child looked at him with blunt surprise and ran off.

Eventually, after showing his feather to a friend and then to a neighbour, the man became so sad at their common disbelief that he became sick, and two clean-shaven men in white coats with manicured fingernails came to take him to an asylum. Ever persistent, yet losing courage, he held on tightly to his fragile sign of hope. He showed it to a guard and to an inmate. Once again he was not believed.

Eventually the man died with bitter disappointment and unassuaged grief in his heart, hunched over his angel's feather,

"All the saints live in asylums now," whispered my host as we left the theatre.

From Holland I flew to Oslo where I met with my husband, and on to Italy's northern alpine valleys with their lovely opportunities for clear-aired hill climbing, snug terracotta rooftop views, and the little baroque churches which seemed strangely out of place in this landscape of fresh rusticity and homely geranium-studded *pensions*.

Despite the wonderment I had felt at exploring Oslo, seeing the Gokstad ship and Ibsen's apartment, not to mention my beautiful and refreshing sojourn in Italy, I carried sadness in my heart at the fate of the misunderstood and dying dreamer clutching the feather of an angel.

At one of Milano's vast airports on the way back to Australia, I bought a book to read on the flight home. 'The Heart of the Hunter' appeared to be just the right length to last until Tokyo, plus waiting time at Tokyo Airport, and for most of the ongoing flight to Sydney.

I did not yet know that within the pages of the *Laurens van der Post* book there lay a compassionate refrain to the sad song of the puppet play. The author tells a story, related to him by a Hottentot, of a hunter of the Bushman people of South Africa who visited a place of beauty, where birds sang by deep water, to fill his calabash with drinking water. There he sees the reflection of a huge, unfamiliar white bird. He quickly looks up, but the bird has already vanished over the treetops.

Restless and unable to forget the experience, he leaves his family to travel into the great world beyond. To travel is no hardship for a Bushman, yet at every place he visits he hears rumours of the bird, but nothing of substance.

At last, old and weary, he is told he will find the bird atop a great mountain, in the heart of Africa, far away from his original home. He seeks out the mountain and begins to climb, on and on, until he finds himself on the edge of the snowline. There is no sign of this most marvellous of birds, or any bird at all. Realising the end may be near and feeling he has failed, he throws himself down onto the mountainside, calling "Oh, my mother!" A voice answers him, telling him to look up. He does so.

> *...in the red sky of a dying African day, a white feather (was) falling slowly down towards him...He held out his hand and grasped it. With the feather in his hand, he died content as night fell.* *

Nearly one hundred pages further on, at the very end of the book, an illustration depicts a white feather that is held by the hand of the Bushman as he dies.

I am greatly comforted and inspired as I look out of the plane window as the rays of the new sun break upon the ochres and reds of the Australian earth.

Joanna Jaaniste

* *Laurens van der Post* 'The Heart of the Hunter', Vintage Classics London & Sydney, 1961

"How much interest do we take in the other? Are we interested in the other? Interest brings warmth and light to the soul. How much warmth and light there would be in the world if we all made the time to take an interest!"

Norma Blackwood

The Pest

I found him fully made, a nuisance at first,
Grabbing for the sun by day or silent
Moon at night, between time and money,
Near flowers and trees and animals who pulled him
Along in their urgent spurt to maturity.
His long limbs carried him for miles
Without fatigue, as by magic.

On our endless drives looking for
A place to live or die, we saw
Little houses set back from busy
Highways carrying at dusk the weekend
Trippers to their cities. Inside,
Fading into night, the old, forgotten
And the poor huddled up again to get
Unneeded sleep for another day. But
His green eyes saw the world as a future
Paradise already here, the flaws
Dispersed by dreams, the gaps by deepest sleep.

Somehow he knew the woes of totally
Forgotten people. When he looked in the mirror
He saw himself with wings.

Robert Gurry-Zentner

I am surrounded by angels

They lie scattered on the carpet, across the bedspread,
along the windowsill. Christmas light picks out gold
and silver foil. They arch like seahorses, trumpets at their lips.

Cockatoos rise from graves like gargoyles, hard cries
rip the air, coxcombs flex, wings extend with thoughts of flight,
Their sharp faces deny the ecstasy a chisel had imparted.

Above Arden Street white birds wheel at night, pass from
        blackened sky
To tissue cloud, from luminescence to invisibility. Where do they go,
And what possessed their brief anarchic play?

A parachute is a breath of grace. It floats so there's no fixed point
to judge its height or speed. A paraglider hold nylon lines,
wills them to lift him higher, grips so he skims the bay.

I've angels on a blue silk shirt. I wear them
ironically. They have no body or one that is apparent.
Angels are pure bright gems: men are made of clay.

A man is bicycling down Clovelly Road. His face is set. He
        wears glasses,
a teardrop helmet and, as though he doubted and expected
he could fly, he pedals towards the quick edge of the cliff.

Brook Emery

The day I ran away from home

You'd think that being the only child in a house full of grown-ups I would get plenty of attention but it seemed that the only time anyone took any notice of me was when they wanted to complain about something I'd done. I decided I'd had enough and I was going to teach them a lesson.

I went and told them, one by one, that I was going to run away from home right then and made a big thing of going around and gathering my favourite toys and tying them with wool on my three-wheeler out on the front lawn.

The grown-ups all dutifully filed out on the front verandah to watch me make my departure but unfortunately no one rushed out on the front lawn to drop on their knees and beg me to stay.

Not giving up hope, I pushed my three-wheeler out on the footpath and looked back to see if someone had decided that they couldn't live without me and was rushing across the front lawn to come and plead with me to return, but no, they were all standing in a line on the front verandah smiling at me and calling out goodbye as they also waved with their handkerchiefs. At this point my grandfather said something in disgust and walked back into the house.

This wasn't turning out the way I'd expected, but in my pride I decided that I'd already committed myself so I'd better get on with it.

I got on my trika and manfully started to peddle off. However, this was when my toys started to drop off and I had to stop every few feet to tie one or another of them back on. At one point I looked back and the grown-ups left on the verandah had their hands over their mouths and seemed to be shuddering.

I almost reached the end of the street when I heard someone running behind me. I turned around just in time to see Mum thunder up to me and then felt a sharp pain as she slapped me across the arm after which she started dragging me back home with the injunction,"Don't ever do that to me again."

Nobody said another word about it but I decided I'd never try it again. However, the next year, I did, and I got a little further that time.

Darryl Reid

you can't see him for dust

kickstarted by his Tribe's
fragmentation
the small brown-eyed boy greedily
sniffs up vapour from the pink fuel

backfiring   this mini Molotov cocktail
rockets his budding cognition
and Dreamtime consciousness
into Never-Never Land

Felicity Daphné Baldry

No exit

Fighting my way to sleep,
I paused, looked down:

there around the curve of the boulder
a portion, at least, of the sea –

a grey, outstanding stillness. If there were
whitecaps I couldn't see them,

breakers would have been hidden
beneath the ledge I stood on.

Daub-painted sea, with just enough
of the start of eternity to strike fear in

my navel. But there, on the right,
the sheer wall of granite

occluded periphery by half.
Move, move – but how? – mind

made the leap,
to the beach below.

Different climate, the sea
bluer now,

vastness of ocean unhindered
by blinders at either eye.

Stay down here, then.
But no, no

good –
back to the boulder

on waking's precipice,
the closed-off side of me,

angry,
the north coast sealed.

Richard Deutch

The night before

There are things
sometimes
hard to remember,
like the place I was
trying to go to
last night.

The fog on the other side
of the lake is as dense as the cloud
that was blackening
my head
last night.

Mario Licon Cabrera

Motels

Not quite far enough towards the dream,
not quite near enough to call home,
their beacons are suspended animation, intangibility,
a harmless enough stasis.
Yet some among us who are told we've made safe
ground,
release their hold too soon, and fall,
there, for the camera, in Nobody's Room,
a final smudge against the canvas,
stopping for the night,
before, we or they, are ready.

Danny Gardner

Betwixt

The rock
closest to the hard place
bears the imprint
of many hands

and holds the souls
of those who fell between.

Ann Davis

Hamlet would have known

Hamlet would have known
how it felt up there on Kings Tableland:
winds whipping trees and scrub
below the ramparts
churning treetops
far as my eye could see.

Could've been blown over the edge
or jumped
taken others with me
gone with the flow
over the top
into the abyss
ended troubles
not opposing but embracing
all or nothing
found God...

Not this time

To be.

Pip Griffin

"If at first you don't succeed, maybe skydiving is not for you."

Yuri

taught
needlework and p.e.
in a convent
36 years
one day
she
sold her morris minor
dark
green
single owner
immaculate condition
and went to america
to marry mr knight
twice widowed
her pen-pal of 5 years
they were happy
i like to think
for 18 months
until he died
he was 72
i would like
to touch
you
why is it
nobody minds
if you look
or think desire
but if suddenly
you reached out and touched your desire
it wouldn't be right

lying in bed
i watch the fan
spin slow
i think i
could touch the
edge of its petals
and they would
feel like feathers

Ten Ch'in Ü

"What's wrong with Sydney? In Poland, they would have taken them."

Bogdan Koca complaining after his car was broken into and thieves took his car radio but not a stack of poetry books.

"Life drawing class led me to a fascination with portraits, and to a broader understanding of the human body, my own included. It also led to a search for a faster medium, thus began my love affair with ink. I love its challenge and freshness, and its honesty. Using ink I quickly learnt to value my mistakes. There is no way to hide them."

Pat Pillai introducing her work at a Live Poets Society night

The Boat House
(Laugharne)

Green hills slope to the sea
a beached boat on a bed of seaweed
the sweep of a bird in flight
the screech of a gull
and fish rising.
Undercurrents –
eddies and swirls of dark water
echo of men's voices
from the village pub where he spent his mornings.

Then home to lunch with Caitlin –
and poetry.

Unfit for war service
he relived his childhood in documentaries:

The park next to his house
and the Lane of Confidence
where the boy told secrets.
At grammar school -
words singing in his heart -
he sneaked out
and was sprung by the Head:
"Where are you going, Thomas?"
"Home to write poetry."
"Well, don't get caught."

Once he flew up to the window
and the music teacher
knocked over metronome.
I follow the cliff path
climb the stile into a meadow
with buttercups, white daisies
rabbits, and a blackbird singing.
The ruins of the fishermen's church
teeter above the sea wall
like a broken bird.

In 1953 Dylan dies
of *an insult to the brain.*
Outside his boathouse
water closes in
as the swift tide turns.

Hilarie Lindsay

Adrift

Crowded
Rotting timbers creak
Stinking motor splutters
Vast blues
The boat rocks
No, it is my mind

Jacqueline Buswell

Letter while flying

The world's reduced to a cabin window,
now seacoast, now cloud, now interrupted
sandy tracks under foreshortened trees, and height is
more dislocation than detachment, the uneasy trust
that must be given to technology if we wish to escape
the down below. It's smooth at 30,000 feet.

I've decided, I mean to tell you, I hate flying too.
It's the take-off, the way the engines tense themselves
and charge, the same and opposite as abandonment
to a wave – there's no contact going up, apart from;
not like going down and into. Flying's a cryogenic state,
straight-line stimulation, the brain cells dropping out
as air filters in. I hope there's more to death than this.

You know the way sparrows flying in formation
suddenly agree to make patterns of their own,
then just as suddenly coalesce as though their many bodies
had a single mind or at least a single purpose?
Perhaps we look like that to birds, distance lending shape
to randomness. No matter how connection
attenuates, originality can only be defined
as degrees of unravelment from the flock.

It's different on a plane, a rigid pattern has been imposed
by need. It's silly to kick against necessity or the
obviousness of thought, the way it flukes and flits.
Billy Wilder had ten rules for making films.
Rules one through nine: don't be boring. Rule ten,
I forget. Where does that leave Beckett,
Proust, big chunks of Joyce or almost
any thought – I'm scared to think of poems, at best
third-rate philosophy someone said. Writing about

thinking about thinking by writing of something else.

I see no alternative to this trajectory. We'll land,
brakes straining to absorb the re-connection.

Brook Emery

jacaranda house

forties bloated worn blotched aggro
she exits the shut-open-shut door
jacaranda house - drug and alcohol service
on elizabeth street - subtle as a train smash

she re-enters her waiting circle family
women only   they open to let her in
stand silent round their tattoo'd demon
methadone leaks down inside her

a smile wells up   two words float out
"less go"   she rolls off   their signal
they follow   pushing a baby stroller
and carrying ragged shopping bags

a twelve-year-old brings up the rear
chatting away on her mauve mobile

Bill Tibben

Little Swallow

We share a destiny:
wandering between hemispheres.
You with your comrades
and I by myself,
seemingly alone,
but not so,
having many friends.

You appear each spring
in the sky
and fly within your group,
having crossed the great ocean,
swallow, tiny little swallow.

And when the autumn mists descend,
you are on your way again.
The distant North,
your other homeland, calls,
swallow, little swallow.

In both lands
you build a nest,
a new home.
I too am building my nest,
a new home in my old age.

But really I am homeless
though, strangely, everywhere at home.
My true home is not on this earth
but in the heavens.

Susan Haris

A Window to the Sea

The river submerses me
I am the earth's passionate fruit
the wind inscribes its melodies
upon my face
my sight roams this vastness
the earth turns to my hand
that merrily holds the seasons
by wind and rain and flowers and fields.
With my hand I raise the stars
release them in the heavens
that I may celebrate the distance.

Once
I was the forest
beginning in the branches
a master in the plant kingdom
carrying the tops of the trees upward
and sleeping like a bird
guarded by the breeze.

Once
I was the caves and the rocks and the valleys
and preceded by my caution in the animal kingdom
with my fire which I lit with a stone
to change my voice.

And once
I was the fields in the plains of the world
blossoming with my comely fingers
and upright back
lashed by whips that I fed bread
to fatten
and I become slimmer
and avenge myself.

Now
I have completed my life's cycle
cracked by steel wheels
filled by oil
clotted by carbon
overwhelmed by mud
lead lies in my blood
and stones pull me.

I completed my life's cycle
to open a window on the sea
and race the wind.

Shawki Moslemani
Translated from the Arabic **Papers of Solitude**
by *Raghid Nahhas* and *Noel Abdulahad*

"In my recent work I combine ink, collage and mixed media techniques often with words buried or semi-obliterated in the process. The basis of my collage relies on threads from the edges of torn canvas, and discarded dress patterns. The way I am working feels more like writing a poem, following some pre-ordained rhythm in the brain that keeps shaping and reshaping until the desired image appears. I am exploring layers, now building them up from discarded material, instead of pulling them apart. I hope that my work might open a window for the viewer to the multi-layered nature of reality as I see it."

Pat Pillai

Horse Opera

1. Country Matters

Long faces nosing over stable doors,
a line of trophy heads and watchful eyes;
shifting haunches, the hum of piss and straw;
horse-whiff, ancient must, oiled saddle leather.

Old sweat-twisted *tack*. I've heard the word, it fits
what's trestle-slung or perched on pegs; leather
tongues those *yah-yah* girls fiddle through clasps;
country matters; stirrups, girths notched tight.

The bustle of big fillies - all teeth and arse
and whip. Shrug off my worn old biker leathers,
flicked crop juddering against my plastic boots,
and in borrowed jodpurs, not quite Mr. Darcy

but, good thighs and bollocks, I can strut
through breeding, flesh - appreciate a damn good seat.

2. Spurs

The bit's shine frothed and crusted green: this big
shy face, a secret whispered in her ear.
So many hands of new and nervous mare
- eighteen, nineteen? I wouldn't know, but *huge*.

Saddle up, then lead her out. And at the box,
check girth for slippage, the stirrups' notch.
Swing leg over, mount. Take up the slack.

Thumb frayed reins. She's slow, grumping back
to straw, the water pail... I kick,
she snorts, clops into a disgruntled trot.

Thwack her useless bump and grind, but the crop
can't fire her. Slide out the stirrups.
The stable-hand distracts her with a carrot,
fits shiny traps to my bootheels. Spurs.

3. Achilles

Orthopaedic. Clean as surgical steel.
She's already nervy before he's clamped
Achilles braces round my plastic heels.

And off again. I'm careful, angling ankles
in and out. Correct her head. Relax.
Find the hot, sweet spot that gears her canter.

Lean back into the roll and go.
She finds the drumbeat of her own long stride,
stretches out against her shadow.

Crouching over the mane's disorder,
twitching ears as half a ton of muscle takes flight,
takes the stile, jumps into grace. Glides.

Out of control, she's jumping everything in sight.
I'm holding on, despite the spurs' sly bite.

Cliff Forshaw

That day's walk

The day he left
his fingers remained on the lock
his feet on the sidewalk
a layer of skin over the asphalt

Is this a walk or a death?
they asked, and when he
lifted his arms, they said
that he was trying to fly
but he was only waving
goodbye to his face

Wadih Sa'adeh
Translated from the Arabic by *Sargon Boulus*

Letter to a friend

Are you never coming back?

Remember, is it the eclipse or the rising sun?
You must have lost and found your way through woods
as I have done.
Sometimes we have sprinkled seeds
upon our little earth,
grown a jungle where we search
for ways, and losing, found
the fruits.

Journeys never end on earth,
horizons move,
each day deters the finishing line.
We are not puppets strung
nor dead dreams hung
like laundry.
We have living to do.
Who am I
and who are you?

Dominique Yap

red guitar

"In death lies a stupendous knowing. But
the point is to possess it while living."

Albert Steffen

Summer Night
(After Rilke)

On nights like this
my sister grows,

who was here once, and died.
She was very little.

Since then,
many nights have passed.

She must be very beautiful.
Soon a man will marry her.

Richard Deutch

Midwinter

I've settled in to watch the garden,
it's what I do most days.
Dead limbs falling from the trees,
not many birds around,
wind-blown leaves and weeds
on the verandah where I sit.
The sea is always in the distance.

I bought myself a pot from a shop
in the city. Taiwan fingers shaped it.
It's filled with silk flowers.
Dust on the petals turned them dark and sad.
I can think them any colour I choose.
I can multiply them if I think of bees.
I could count the petals, count the leaves.
I could die from longing.

Paula McKay

Umbopo-Shilling-Boy

Sometimes when I sit alone at my desk
and look out on the world through my window,
musing perhaps on a new poem, I think

of all the years it's taken to get there
and I ask myself where have they all gone,
the roaring boys, the girls with sun-bleached hair?

Dimly remembered faces, time-faded,
lost. Are they now joined to the silent dead?
And I think of Umbopo-Shilling-Boy

selling newspapers in Adderley Street
in bare feet, patched pants, torn shirt and beanie
shouting "Argie" in the blunt South-Easter,

with a grin as wide as a hand-saw, bright
on his swart face and then I ask myself
why I should remember his strident voice

among so many voices from the past
and think perhaps I've missed something, somewhere.
But I know I haven't. The paper boy

no longer shouts his wares. The wind still blows.
Poems have a habit of falling apart.
I sit before my window looking out.

Don Rowley

Maria and Henry

Maria with hands as white as the whey
Maria with sunglasses
Maria with a confidence
Maria with Henry
in an olive orchard
lunch
time

Henry with Maria
and a crippled timelessness
fading like a final sequence
like dusk
like

Henry and Maria
with empty cups
against their silent lips
with Henry's eyes by-passing
Maria's sight
with not a single sigh
of breeze
so soft
so cool
so full of insipidity
at the break of noon

Maria with a rose
between two handsome fingers
Maria with a scent of thyme
and marjoram

Maria with Henry
who with hazy eyes
dreams about Maria
that she's never been

Maria with common needs
and common face
Maria with plans
and a corn-flowered blouse
Maria with smile
Maria with shoes
awaiting further stroll

Maria with Henry
musing next to her

Henry with splash of Brut
over his chin
Henry with Maria in the empty room
Henry with hands and arms so able
Henry that has never been

Maria with a leaf of parsley in her mouth
Maria with a plastic comb
and with a ring
that mourns the past

Maria with dawn
between her arms
Maria with shadows of
half broken blinds

Maria with Henry
in a looking glass

Henry and Maria
that have never been

Bogdan Koca

Shadow Stalker
(to Maria Trefely-Deutch, my mother,
who is greatly missed)

Today we all sat around a fire as if to
stare it down what would Jack think nothing
but all he feels in is pain but what does
madam think of what has transpired here but
all was lost and forgotten in a whisper
from me to you but all seems to fade and
die but not forgotten.
Left behind steps on his shadow as he
steps, falls and cries and stepped to the
day he died at that it leaves to stalk
another with Jack, envy, fire and madam,
forget the times when Jack, fire and envy
were happy it stood tall on a street corner
but no one wanted to notice or accept its
being at the time it left but remembered its
pain and loss to live another day as Jack did.

David Joseph Deutch

Crusoe

(Very loosely after the Spanish of Tomás Segovia
Todo hombre sin mujer es un Crusoe.)

Without a woman, this man's a Crusoe,
shipwrecked by absence, decked by the gruesome
sham of drudgery: the unwinsome, lose some,
lose some more; the how-so? This whoso

dares spins out of control, barrelling bone
-white dunes. He hates the Eden between the waves,
sown with trans-ocean spores, broken wings, tail-fin. Alone,
a tattered palm for his flag, unwashed, unshaven. Not saved.

No big fat juicy fruit plopping off the trees.
No dog, umbrella, effing parrot, shady shack.
No Friday footprints, whisky, cheeky monkeys.
No Shakespeare, Bible, luxury item. No eight all-time killer tracks.

Strike out for sunwink, thrash surf, hit that swell's blue rise.
Hope to crash up, beached: Tahiti, a coast of sandy thighs.

Cliff Forshaw

Vacant Situation

To be exact, there is a vacancy,
But one we can't afford to advertise.
It follows us around our empty rooms.
That's why it isn't in the prestige space
We took last week, but thanks for your enquiry.

There was this woman, asking from the blue
If we could bear to see her. I was free,
As I supposed, so why not interview her?
Come in, I said, I'll introduce my colleagues,
on neither side is there any obligation.

The sort of person we've been looking for
Will give support, illumine what is dark
In our conceptions, give some credibility
To our great scheme, as yet unformulated,
Scarcely, indeed, beyond the planning stage.

Should you decide to give me this assignment,
She said, you have my new address. My flight
Number is somewhere in a clear domain.
I have declared some simple gifts at Customs.
I'm glad we had this talk. I'll wait outside.

We took too long with our deliberations.
The emptiness walks round with us forever.

John Miles

The Telephone Always Rings in My Absence

when email comes my computer is not on
when I miss someone someone is not there
but when someone is there my thoughts are elsewhere
I want the rain but no water comes
when I am thirsty and hungry I am always alone
the bookshops are always overstocked with books
and you don't feel like saying anything about the rubbish
littering the ground although you do
I am never in any mood to watch television
and I feel let down after reading fiction
when I go out I have to shut two doors and lock up three locks
when I go to the market I go past the vegetable stands several times
if I keep close to the telephone and the mobile phone for a whole day
        they just won't ring
then I keep close to the bed the window the grey sky
and a boring and unending interest in the words
it's only when an earthquake occurs that I discover that people
        can die
and that all the predictions have become pursuing reports
when I think of calling someone someone is not there
and when I think of calling someone's beeper I find that
        someone doesn't have it
when the answering machine asks me to leave a message
I wait a little then hang up
the worst helpless feeling is that
I want to find someone but don't want to find someone
knowing that I do but don't admit to it
this way of living

Ouyang Yu

The Oldest Band in the World

On Saturday afternoons,
in *The Hero of Waterloo*,
The Oldest Band in the World
makes the climb to the stage
and plays dance-hall and jazz.
In the cool, subdued chamber,
where hands count out
small change for shandies,
first, only light
floods the stone
with arrival, departure.
The band taps out elegant pathways—
slow weaves of gesture-through-tune—
show-turns that bear what remains
of the body's lost fires.
They keep perfect time
and they walk through old shorthand for passion.
The red guitar trembles but transitions happen.
The pianist's body has curled
to a crumpled bass clef
but keeps darting out licks.

Once, they led straight to love's blood sports,
these heart-coded curves that a whole nation knew.

Now, they are strangely-closed gateways —
   counting away,
through the clockwise of honeycombed light.

Martin Langford

Birdcage
(After Saint-Denys-Garneau)

I'm a cage
a birdcage
a bone cage

the bird inside my bones is death
piecing its nest together

when it's quiet you hear his wings flutter

when you laugh then suddenly stop
you hear him deep inside you
a tiny bell

the caged bird death in my bones

Why doesn't he fly away?
Can you catch him?
Can I?
what

He won't leave until he eats my heart
the fist of blood with my life inside it

his wild eyes
my soul in his beak

Richard Deutch

Tonight

This expanding moon illuminates
not the solitary curve of a cat's back but
a page touring as fast as light in which a poet
named *Gonzalo Rojas* explodes
in a parsimonious and celebratory excess remembering
the first one hundred years of a Library that was a man,
a man named *Borges.*

Slightly open the door and silently step out to stare at the moon.
The cat is now a two-headed spinning dragon spreading names
and dates that exist only on the *nervatures* of the leaves
of Funes' memory.

The cat could be the same that once jumped
on the lifeless chest of *Billy the Kid*
and the dragon a hydra
or the rooster that used to carry the aurora on his beak:
a knife the beak and *A Book of Sand* the moon.

Mario Licon Cabrera

Heart

bird
flies
into the sky of the other
returns
consummately
alone

Ten Ch'in Ü

Prague Birds

I The Swan

Despite the Encyclopædia Britannica,
I never die.

If it appears I'm caught by scrutiny,
I simply swim and mingle with the others.

Indistinguishable,
only
a slightly deeper bending of the neck,
a little dirtier, the plumage of a failed aristocrat.

Once every hundred years
I lay a golden egg.
It hatches quickly
and a fetid sigh escapes.

A sifting of my guts would find
that history cannot be digested.

I swim under the Charles Bridge
on which the people cross from side to side.
Sometimes I dunk my head
and see the bones of John Nepomuk,
Saint…
I take my breadcrumbs where I find them.

Some in-the-know
have thought me an enchanted princess.

Well,
that suits me fine.

II The Pigeon

Under the dust
and the soot from the coal stoves
all of us are white,
like flour,
like virgin snow.

But early on
we acquired a taste for breadcrumbs.
Now we gather in the great square daily,
circle benches, peck and hustle.

Our homelessness
has made us lawless,
disrespectful;
we soil without a thought
the blessed heads of martyrs.

We are common
we admit.
But look at rats
who, having lost their wings,
sink even lower.

Us younger ones
inherited this dirt.
We can't be blamed.
We are like rags for wiping windowsills.

It takes a heavy rain
to wash the years away.

It's rare,
but sometimes
when the sky is grey

a human being looks up
and thinks he's seen a dove.

III The Peacock

I am the queen's great favourite,
she loves me more then all the others.

My tail is like the rainbow that fulfils her grief.

I am too beautiful for freedom.
So she keeps me in her secret garden
surrounded by four walls of stone.

I wander through a maze of briars
pretending to be lost to please her.

With my great wings
I could escape,
but then,
what would I do out in the dirty streets?

I keep them folded like a fan.

They say my queen is old,
her death is imminent.
But what's a rumour?

The Spring is coming and the briars soften.
She will come for me one night.
With all my hundred eyes
I stay awake to greet her.

IV The Raven

I prefer the leafless trees in winter
and the barrenness of stone.

I have perched atop the spires
when the bells were pealed at coronations,
and followed with my quick black eyes the funeral processions.

I have watched from windowsills
the alchemist's nocturnal vigils, seen
his crucible of gold,
his carbon heart.

I don't excuse my habits.
Everything belongs to death
and all of us are scavengers.

I have observed
that battle scenes look different from above,
but even close up corpses are anonymous.
I have observed
that children die like parents,
men like women.

When I fly I feel the hunger of the grave.

My heavy head is like a paperweight,
it keeps men's thoughts from scattering -
memento mori.

The winters here are cold,
but night is kind to me
and hides me in her pocket like a dagger.

Jakob Ziguras

Permitted without stopping

We stop
among the words as if
they are the destination
when they flag the direction.

Yet the dog would
arch into inflections
to include himself in the family round.

Herrooow! Oooohrrr!
Hello! I am here, too.
Can we go for a walk?

And the gods
wear our faults to mask
their identity.

In the man
in the woman
gods travel incognito.
Let us speak their parts.

Gods and dogs covet our quirky estate.
Such is the situation, folks!

My body is thinking of your body.
Can we lie together
if our truths cannot?

Does God lie to (His) God?

The half moon tonight looks like
a half moon. Oh, if you must,
like a bowl of brightness
tilted over to the right.

In the world of appearances
we cannot always find
what we are looking for;
but once we know it is there
suddenly we can see it.

Kangaroo paw plant jacks out
stems, red furred
flowers.

You beloved,
child, man, woman:
to possess you
is not the point.

What bird squiggled shit
on my Subaru boot?

Thrub! Nightcat jumps
on fence.
Face like an old-fashioned
movie star sweetheart.

Monty nosing another pee-reeked bush
misses the fence-sitter altogether.

Mirror
dreamshape within my grasp
wobbles into definition
discloses a form, disappears.

A brown splotched rabbit hops
into your garden moonbright.

So easy slip between the cracks
of the other's inattentions.

You. It was you who
stuffed up the animal
of our love.

It was I who could
not inhabit the supple
body of life.

Syntax locates epiphany.

Be where the currents are.
Upswell and downswoon.
If you swim in the shallows,
don't complain the sand rubs.

To make a poem
unmake
a poem.

God is a verb.

You can't step back
into something you had.
You can, until suddenly
it's different.
It was the same and the same and changing
and (but it was always happening),
you are at another place.

Otherness is slippery.
Otherness is.

Cadence takes precedence.

My body is subtle with
new substances.

Possession is nine-tens of the flaw.

There is no cure for heartache.
The cure is that which
caused the
heart
to break.

Open and shut haste.

I came out so far to meet you
I can't find my way back.
There is no self
to come back to.

Ten Ch'in Ü

Flag-tailed Bird of Paradise

(George W. Bush instructed the enemy to hold up white flags and stand twenty metres away from their tanks, promising that if they did, they would be spared.)

Thought to be extinct, they are appearing
through the red mist, their white tails waving at blunt
helicopters splattering the earth. These creatures
from paradise play dead when attacked -
they freeze, clamped to a branch,
the tiny flags of their tails
barely shimmering in broken sunlight.
They once lived in jungles on islands in the Pacific,
but haven't been found dead there since 1958.
Some escaped to Arabia: sold to collectors and bred
in captivity, they were taken up by zoos,
kept in palaces and inbred. Flunkies fed them
and sultans hovered about them, marvelling at how they
became extraordinary in their deformities, their
cream-coloured plumage shot through with
pale, beautiful rainbows, their eyes enormous,
pink, and their tail-flags heavy - almost too heavy
to hold up, but not theirs to withhold.

Robert Adamson

Bondage

A friend gives me
a bonsai tree,
I think of Chinese girls
with feet bound
into lotus feet
to fit into a husband's hand
and of young English girls
with smelling salts
for fainting fits
from whalebone corsets,
tightly laced
wasp waists
to fit a husband's collar.

Today the dwarf tree is on its side
as if escaping from the pot.
If I should offer
it release,
find it a spot in my front garden,
would I wake a sleeping giant
who seeks revenge
with tangled branches spreading wide,
the garden in perpetual shade?

Instead I trim the dwarfed tree's roots,
pinch back the parody of branches,
consign it to its stunted world.

Hilarie Lindsay

My Mother's Song

Returning to New Zealand
shipboard with parents, brothers, sisters
from Tahiti where they'd lived a year in 1910
while Grandfather built houses for white people,
they sang around the piano nightly.

The Herr Doktor revealed he was a singing teacher
said she should be trained to sing in opera
he would take her with him to Vienna –
such talent could not be denied.
The cost? All would be taken care of.

Grandfather, of course, said no.
She was too young, too gentle, too naïve,
too shy, too nervous.
He had other plans for her: a suitable job, a safe
        marriage.
There was no more to be said.

We have one photo of her wedding day
thin then, pretty, with a veil and train,
my father and the family proud beside her.

I never knew her parents, dead when I was born.
What happened to her brothers, those fine boys?
Her sisters lived nearby
visited when I was growing up
as did my father's brothers and their wives.
Jim was the only one she ever mentioned:
killed in Italy, 1916.

The mother I knew cared for her children
then her ailing husband.

Loyal.
Past buried.
Life half-lived.

I never heard my mother sing.

Pip Griffin

Offering

Laugh
now with your dissolved teeth
into the obscure earth's womb.
Laugh
now with your skull-flowering fountain
far from everything that you were.
Laugh
with a jaw beating right and left,
with ironic mussitation; like a shooting star,
as a lightning sets aside sorrows and
with a sweet smile, still shine to all the cardinal points.
Laugh
then from the last and most profound corner
where you have arrived.
You and you and you and all
those dear dead ones that one day lived
here laughing with me.

Mario Licon Cabrera

"What is *mussitation*? Something, say it in a very low voice." *Mario Licon Cabrera*

sometimes, eternity

"A man sets himself the task of portraying the world. Over the years he fills a given surface with images of provinces and kingdoms, mountains, bays, ships, islands, fish, rooms, instruments, heavenly bodies, horses, and people. Shortly before he dies he discovers that this patient labyrinth of lines is a drawing of his own face.

Jorge Luis Borges
Translated by *Kenneth Krabbenhoft*
'Selected Poems' ed. *Alexander Coleman*

Sand-glass Grain by grain the days pass and
I remember every second of this beautiful story.
The echo of your warm voice heard only yesterday
remains delicious to my enchanted ear. Melodies of
folkloric songs, ritornello, still rock me mellow
bar to bar, without possibly ignoring the
flamboyant red balustrade
of bougain
villea,
and
the
ph
i
l
tre
of
love
disguised
as a nightcap.
At dawn lips meet.
Conquered with love
in the clasp of your arms:
tender, radiant, I am eternally
your faithful lover. *Telly Nakhdjavani-*
Hall Translated from the French with *Ten Ch'in Ü*

Ubique

When?

Does it matter?
Does anything matter?

That's not an argument.
Yes, it does matter.
It matters that it did.
It matters that it did and,
in a magic second,
pushed away the walls.

Why were walls there in the first place?

A-a-a-a-h.

A-a-a-a-h?

It's a recognised convention that means
who knows?

But you know don't you? You know.

A-a-a-a-h.

David Morris

The Water List

The wine list was extensive
though the house wine
(like a good housewife)
merited no description.

There was a mellow red
a feisty wine
with a good length
the flavour of berries
and the aroma of autumn.

The pick of the crop
had the warmth of sunshine
the hint of peach blossom
the sweetness of a ripe melon
the smile on winter's face.

I waved aside the wine list
"Could I see the water list?"

"We have sparkling or still,"
the waiter said.

My mind conjured up the water list.

Water with the hint of spring
from snow melting at the thaw.
Water from a secret source
deep in the earth
heavy with minerals.

River water
gushing over a cliff
into a deep pool

at the bottom of a fern-lined gorge
to emerge as a sunlit stream
bubbling
over smooth polished pebbles.

The waiter gave a discreet cough.

I woke from my reverie,
"Bring me a carafe of tap water
with the taste of tadpole."

Hilarie Lindsay

Offered to his Wife
Li Bai

Eighteen score days each year…
Day in, day out, you see me getting tipsy:
I soak it up, as would a sod of clay,
till drunken as a lord, your Lord Muck!
Although you are a poet's wife, married to
        "Far-Too-Pure",
what odds, I ask you? Would you be better off
if wedded to a pontiff – "Far-Too-Often"?

Translated from the Chinese by *Rene Manning*

"Life, like me, is too short to resist."
Telly Nakhdjavani-Hall

The Caretaker's Aria

Seal up the floor,
Seal up the floor,
That's what my special
Sealer is for.

Seal in the future,
Seal in the past,
Watertight sealers
Are meant to last.

In every staffroom
There's a squealer
Who must be fixed
With foolproof sealer:

The head struts round
With his posh degree,
But I'm the one
With the master key.

John Miles

John: "It's all maths, everything is maths."
Aya: "No, everything is art!"
John: "No! It is all artistic mathematics."

John Blackwood recounting a conversation with a student.

Before I Sleep

You have faded now
faded from me
surely.
But that is only distance,
that is only space
only.
You have faded now
through space only,
slowly.
But that is only distance,
that is only space
only
space.
You have faded now
but not in warmth and gentleness,
not in lingering spirit.
With your presence close,
drawing closer,
surely,
through the distance,
slowly, closely,
we talk before I sleep.
We talk through fading distance
but that is only space
only.
We talk before I sleep,
through space
slowly
through only distance
only,
surely.
You have faded now
faded from me

surely.
But that is only distance
that is only space
only
space.

Sue Hicks

Eagle
(In the manner of Ted Hughes)

The people say the emperor has a palace
to parade his pompous greed.
But the people misunderstand.
One of giant stature cannot endure,
is all too constricted by a cottage.
The great soul rightfully requires a great space.
Therefore, I was given the sky,
and do not move in flocks
like the others.

My vision is as sharp as it is wide.
It pierces my victims like a knife.
I make a small circle from a great height.
Turning with the silence of forgotten centuries.
Then, when it suits me,
curve in my wings
and drop like a dart.

Luke Fischer

Rhythm of a Thousand Loaves

sacks upended
bins scooped out
water gushed, trickled in
bowl begins to move
bar stands still
hook spirals it in and out
dough tensioned in, left to rest

now a teaspoon, tablespoon, cup and tiny scale
and when the weighing's done
proportions respected
in goes my finger, round and round
dough tensioned in, left to rest

it grows, they grow
amorphous masses in the long dough trough
and I'll be giddy with
bring 'em back, bring 'em in
bring 'em back, bring 'em in
then cut, hugged
table-deposited
strip-cut for scaling

textures a delight
soft and silken
bubbles burst as hands reclaim
the rhythm of a thousand loaves
'tis too brief, memories crowd in
of night and early light
quietness as ovens roar

living in your limbs
peeling, kneading, rounding, rolling

proud of the handiwork of your hands
crosses cut on light rye cobs
loaves tapped and hollow ringing

Neil Anderson

Bread Fingers

alone at ten pm
she boils two eggs
drinks coffee
does not wash up
licks the butter side of freedom

blank menu

blank page

blink

one egg cracks
the other disembowels itself
becomes egg soup
with a long handled spoon
she eats her three minute silence

Pat Pillai

Night on Mount Ann
(in South-West Tasmania)

The moon has not moved.
A bout of shivering has re-awakened me
To my self-imposed plight:
It means I will survive.

Here I am, in shirt sleeves
With a timing delay on my camera,
Hoping to record the effect
Of heaven's light on the fellow peaks
Bathed in post-midnight glow - far below.

That excuse/idea became my tunnel vision
Assuming I'd need no other nourishment, shelter:
Those things we grow fat on
In self-complete disgust.
For an instant, my memory of indulgent absence of denial
Webs stickily close once more –
Food, wine and argument,
A lover's body curving to make one with my own -
Then the shivering starts again.
Once more I lean against the rock.
Better varicose veins then sleep swallowing me
In a white-out from which I'd probably never return.
Yet - the moon has not moved.

I wait, like an assassin, to pull the shutter's trigger,
Indulge a game that would distract me:
The physical hardship is actually a mere detail.

Danny Gardner

Hope

Falling asleep, he hopes
the wounded around him
calm down,
the wind eases,
the dead depart.

For so long some ships sailed
in his head
and now
he wants to rest.

Shawki Moslemani
Translated from the Arabic **Where the Wolf is**
by *Noel Abdulahad* and *Raghid Nahhas*

Bird

Where do you fly to, bird?
Do you go into your heaven each night?
So that you can be borne to us again in the morning,
Tense with boundless joy,
With your satanic stares, and rude signals,
That bid us stumble from our obsessive rest
And start again.

Danny Gardner

Snorer's Wife

It's like living beside the freeway –
trucks backfire all night
engines rev
slowdown
then speed into top gear.

While I fret over lost sleep,
contemplate murder -
a quick pillow over the face
then bliss,
quiet as a Trappist monastery
(do monks snore?) -
I have only myself to blame,
I leapt into my marriage bed
with my ears open.
Once someone called the police.
Help! Someone being strangled next door!

Only my father-in-law asleep.

Hilarie Lindsay

Cure for Insomnia

Lie on the edge of the bed.
You will soon drop off.

Common knowledge contributed by *Jacques Goldman*

Melissa Magee

I've got a cat called Melissa Magee.
She's a terror to be found,
When she's not chasing goldfish around the bowl
She's prowling butterflies along the ground.

She looked into a mirror one day.
It drove her quite to dismay
'Cause when she looked the look she looked
It looked back the very same way.

She's hot for a tom who passes by.
She goes to waylay him at the gate
But she preens herself so deliciously long
That she always gets there late.

She used to terrorise a bibliophile mouse
Who kept rooms under the stairs,
But with her lumbago, rheumatics and advancing age,
These days she just sits there and glares.

When I looped a bell around her neck
'Cause she was getting in the way, everywhere,
First she scratched then realized it was such a good idea,
Now she rambles, so nonchalant, without a care.

I've a cat called Melissa Magee.
She's a terror to be sure,
When she's not chasing lions around the room
She's lying in wait for them behind the door.

She stares out at the stars at night
From her position on the sill.
Sometimes it's like she's gone out there,

Sometimes I think she will.

She gives me a cuddle late at night
And plays tick-tack on my bed
But I wish she'd go back to her own sweet couch
Instead of sleeping stretched out on my head.

Darryl Reid

A meal

Who is pecking my head
patiently and thoroughly:
the birds of prey
or the birds of slumber?

Shawki Moslemani
Translated from the Arabic **Where the Wolf**
by *Noel Abdulahad* and *Raghid Nahhas*

"Writing - it's a pain on the back! Generally, the poem comes when I am desperately trying to fall asleep. Without a fuss, the words arrange themselves into rhyme on the blackboard of my insomnia."

Telly Nakhdjavani-Hall

Sister's Hands

Tiny hands
made for
caresses and love
bleeding petals
for the sake
of growing buds

Tiny, courageous hands
made for knitting rhythms and rhyme
with stitches of dreams
my hands salute you
sister's hands

Like yours, mine were trapped once
in the cogwheels of life
in the tedious job of survival
looking for independence
working to build a nest
to make it safe

Time was counted in fractions
the same movement repeated a thousand times
eight hours that walked
with iron balls on their feet

The mind crying aloud: "I'm not made for this,
let me free...!"
the spirit running away like a prodigal son
the body remaining still
and the hand...
the hand weeping,
always weeping
for the pen...

Oh, how my hands understand your
Sister's hands...!

Edilia Vidal-Porcu

Note on **Sister's Hands**

This was written in response to **The Hands** by Da-Thao (Que Tran) who came to Australia from Vietnam as a refugee with her three children. Her husband was left behind in Vietnam. A midwife, she had to work in a factory to raise her children because she could not speak English. The author of **Sister's Hands** migrated from Uruguay in 1973 and also had to work in a factory for several years while she was learning English.

Edilia Vidal-Porcu

Optimist

He goes forward two steps
attempts
to drill a hole
in life's wall.

He raises his head
and smiles.

Shawki Moslemani

Translated from the Arabic **Papers of Solitude**
by *Raghid Nahhas* and *Noel Abdulahad*

Fetching Coal

Two months no booze, eight days no cigarettes,
above my head a square of clear blue light.
Fresh snow. All week, the sky's been weirdly bright.
Still feels early, but it's way past eight.

Almost Easter, and this year it's late.
Blue deepens round the big cold moon, the old dead pit.
Snow-melt glows down the mountain. Its trickle competes
with my raspy shovel, the scuttle's settling weight.

Seven, nearly eight months in this place:
fields, rain, mountains, wet sheep, slate.
The dark square of sky-light picked out in fire,
tongues sassing back to the lick in the grate.

Clink in the bunker - from the other end of winter,
the sound of empties still rattling in the crate.

Cliff Forshaw

The Days of Our Lives

The Mystery of the Planet Week

Contemporary Western society regards the old planetary gods of Rome with at best amused indulgence, at worst, ridicule. Yet we are all quite happy to acknowledge them (in combination with their Germanic equivalents) as active in one of the most fundamental aspects of our lives, the names of the seven days of the week.

Beginning with the traditional first day of the week, we have Saturday, Saturn Day; then Sunday (Old High German *sunna)*; Monday, Moon Day (Old High German *mano)*; Tuesday from Tiw the Norse god of war, the Roman equivalent Mars in French Mardi; Wednesday from the Anglo-Saxon god Woden (Norse Odin), the Roman equivalent being Mercury as in French Mercredi; Thursday is obviously Thor's Day, Norse thunderbolt-hurling equivalent of Roman Jupiter thus French Jeudi; and finally Friday, Old High German and Norse Freya, goddess of love (Frigga, another aspect or similar), Roman equivalent Venus as in French Vendredi.

So we have the seven ancient astrological planets of Saturn, Sun, Moon, Mars, Mercury, Jupiter and Venus related directly to the seven days of the week. These are not in the common astrological sequence but in the evolution of the Solar System, and the Earth as described by Rudolf Steiner.

The first incarnation (*manvantara*) of our planetary home he called Ancient Saturn; then following a *pralaya* or spiritual sleep, we have Ancient Sun; then ancient Moon; next the Mars and Mercury Earth (the latter our current planetary state); then future, Jupiter; and finally the future Venus.

Alternative names for the planets have long been provided by Occult Christianity; these are based on the seven cardinal archangels, thus: Saturn-Oriphiel, Sun-Michael, Moon-Gabriel,

Mars-Samael, Mercury-Raphael, Jupiter-Zachariel and Venus-Anael. The colours ascribed to the seven planet-archangels are, in the same order: blue, white, violet, red, yellow, orange and green.

In Steiner circles, there is a profound recognition of the seven days as being ministered to by the seven archangels-planets, hence Saturday is Saturn-Oriphiel Day, Sunday is Sun-Michael Day, Monday is Moon-Gabriel Day, Tuesday Mars-Samael Day, Wednesday Mercury-Raphael Day, Thursday-Zachariel Day and Friday is Venus-Anael day.

As such, many Steiner activities are programmed on days considered blessed by one planet-archangel or another. For instance, regular meetings such as teacher and Society meetings are routinely scheduled on Thursday, Jupiter nominally being the spirit of wisdom, as he is. Arts classes , like eurhythmy, are rather conducted on Wednesday under the auspices of Mercury the quicksilver god of the arts.

Rudolf Steiner went further in detailing the soul-spirit influences active in the week: he divided each of the seven days into four components of approximately six hours each: sunrise to midday, midday to sunset, sunset to midnight, and midnight to sunrise. The seven-four principle is related to soul and body, seven being the numerological number of the soul (the genesis of soul, human and otherwise, is the planets); while the number four is of the body or the Earth, generally.

For this four-in-seven scenario, the planets are in the order, not of the days of the week, but as designated by astrology (or indeed astronomy - but not quite, as we shall see). This is, from an Earth perspective, the three inner planets of Moon, Mercury, Venus, then the Sun around which all seven orbit, then the three outer planets, Mars Jupiter and Saturn. These planets intimately influence the four parts of the day.
But all is not quite as it seems; in the 17th century, in an act of

unconscionable mischief, an attempt was made by the church to discredit astrology by reversing Venus and Mercury; earlier star charts having them in the sequence above. This resulted in all subsequent calculations and deliberations on these two planets being hopelessly corrupted.

In spiritual science we defer to the old sequence, calling them Occults Mercury and Venus; Occult Mercury being the Morning and Evening Star, Occult Venus that tiny planet so rarely seen as it clings to the skirts of the sun. Man may have had the hubris to reverse them, the gods certainly didn't; the forces of Morning and Evening Star Mercury still bestow their arts and sciences benison on an unwitting Earth from the planet the world erroneously calls Venus.

So back to the four parts of the day: starting with Saturday, Saturn ministers to the period sunrise to midday, Moon midday to sunset, Mercury sunset to midnight and Venus midnight to sunrise. Sunday sunrise to midday continues with the Sun, and so on.

Even this rather arcane division is taken into account by many anthroposophists; for instance, I am writing these words on a Friday morning - the Venus-Anael quadrant of the Venus-Anael day. Thus I hope to be inspired by a double injection of the power of Cosmic Love!

As can be seen in the following graph of the 28 (7x4) parts of the week, no two days have the same four planets; remarkable also is the fact that the right planet always starts the day on the right day - rightly speaking! Morning Saturn starts on Saturday, morning Sun on Sun and so on. This is the sequence of Steiner's planetary evolution. In fact, as in the morning sequence though the week, even the columns of the other three parts of the day follow the epochs-days of the week; though each begins with a different planet. For instance the midday to sunset column scrolls down through Moon, Mars, Mercury, Jupiter, Venus,

Saturn, Sun: same order, different starting point. Persuasive evidence of the existence of the Music of the Spheres?

			Dawn to Noon	Noon to Sunset	Sunset to Midnight	Midnight to Dawn
Sat	Saturn	Oriphiel	Saturn blue	Moon violet	Mercury yellow	Venus green
Sun	Sun	Michael	Sun white	Mars red	Jupiter orange	Saturn blue
Mon	Moon	Gabriel	Moon violet	Mercury yellow	Venus green	Sun white
Tue	Mars	Samael	Mars red	Jupiter orange	Saturn blue	Moon violet
Wed	Mercury	Raphael	Mercury yellow	Venus green	Sun white	Mars red
Thu	Jupiter	Zachariel	Jupiter orange	Saturn blue	Moon violet	Mercury yellow
Fri	Venus	Anael	Venus green	Sun white	Mars red	Jupiter orange

Many customary activities in Western culture instinctively (or otherwise) align themselves with one or other planetary parts of the day. We see this in the worship of the Sun God, the Christ, in the morning-Sun quadrant of Sunday. Conversely, Saturday night, the Mercury segment of Saturn Day is usually reserved for entertainment and other festivities: the Saturnalia of Rome was a time of high celebration - Mercury is traditionally fun-loving.

In the light of the above, the reader is invited to reflect on how she or he orders his or her week, and indeed time of day. You might be more in harmony with the Music of the Spheres than you think.

Alan Whitehead

My God,
my good Father,
my eyes are closing,
but yours are open,
watching over me
while I sleep.

As a small child, I sat up in bed every evening before going to sleep, clasped my hands and said this prayer in Hungarian. Now at 80, I wonder whether this is why I can always, anywhere, whether in a tent under the stars or other strange place, fall asleep easily.

Susan Haris

Lamas
in pyjamas
will contemplate the stairs.

Les Wicks

Sometimes, eternity

Stillborn afternoon.

Our love is a flower
which unfolds its beauty
in eternity.

Lallang lush with neglect.

It is unfilial to go mad
in the house of one's parents.
Unseemly to dance in the clothes of marriage.

Attend,
be present at rain falling.

I, who have not sung a note in my life,
not even furtively,
have my mouth open
drinking vowels, supping consonants.

The flowers are easy to paint,
the scent difficult.

The planes have hunted,
hunted.

My pillows flop-lie.
From their dark crinkled nests
swallows rill.

Is your skill that of disappearing
or reappearing?

Flowers must have their consciousness
like breasts.

I only want to walk with you
with no one in between.

Rain in the birdeaten tree.
My friend in the mirror there
poised to break.

Suburban housewife marooned
in eternity of chores, cries, eats,
creates.

Just this present:
to play, press enter now,
and presto! Eternity.

The garden, the whole garden shining with water.

Ten Ch'in Ü

"A novel is long-term commitment. A poem is
a one-night stand. That stands."
Ten Ch'in Ü

Morning Bird

That moment,
that time
when you gave my body
its soul back
and your words,
your gesture
speaking without words,
blessed me
through my body:
how short was that time,
that moment!
How quick
was the morning bird
to announce the arrival
of the end of night!

Assad Cina

Odyssey

Now we have lain together
Now we have lain,
Now we have made our two bodies one, in love
Now we have joined the light of our bodies, with each other
Now our space is one
With the flame of our bodies, in the love,
We take the boat, up the river
With the sun on it,
Take the boat up, under the trees
Take the flowers from the trees
And dress the boat
On the river, to the sun.

And when it gets dark and cold,
The river dark as it grows
We sail on.
And there are fires on the bank,
Fires and people singing.
And we sing the song of the river people
Through the dark, through the night,
Joined to the fire
Of the people singing on the shore.
In the moon, the light of the moon,
The milk of the moon
Spilling on the water
As we sail in the milk-light
Of the sister to the sun,
And our hearts, so close
Our hearts, two birds
Two birds, asleep

Through the dark
Till the birds wake
Till the colours come
Till the light and the colours, and the birds wake,
Till the life comes
With the light on the river.
Till the baby comes out
Shiny head, bright body singing:
It's the birth
When the baby comes,
Hands reaching out for love.

And the beat of three hearts now
The beat of three
Hearts in the light
On the river

But wait…
Look! We have stopped.
Do not be afraid...

We have come
To rest
Upon an island.

Danny Gardner

Dancesong

What stops me now
from going up to you
and taking you in my arms?
Years we wore the quick away.

A morning such as this
could again call up the demons.

Don't sing. Instead let the song
in your throat stream into your arms.
Your legs and feet speak but your arms,
they sing.

Ten Ch'in Ü (speech by *Josephine Porteus*)

Tender Expressions of Interest

What if like the stars
we arrive already dead on this planet
and our troubles, our joys,
all our struggles and activity
are but the delayed registration,
the afterglow
of a longpast illuminated existence
elsewhere?

All the more reason, then,
to make the most exquisite,
the most tranquil,
the most tender
use of our time.

Ten Ch'in Ü

In the Presence of Limestone

Shatterings. Foliated strata, frozen
movement which the kelp unfurls and
furls into the green sea-surge.
Scattered bones, fur and feathers
fluttering among tufts of desiccated
grasses, the little blue flowers
singing to the sky. But limestone…

Hard light brittles on cliff-shards.
Something *zingy* in the air, the skull
resonating with its own. But
what is in that shrill unslaked voice?
That high-tensile sliver of wire
threading through the brain? What is it
cries in us, mainlining this light?

Offshore, the sea's the seals', the breeze
seems definitively to be the gulls'…
The thought's all yours, however,
aching in these white rock formations
also, but still yours. And mine.
And for a moment there, maybe
something in that glances back at us,
a look almost intimate, a longing
also a belonging. Sort of a beholding.

Heady stuff. There you go again,
looking out for some kind of meaning
which just isn't there these days,
significance is *passé,* it's just the sun
baking brains, the sound is called
a migraine coming on. Yeah yeah.
You know all this but find it otherwise:

I will lift up mine eyes unto the hills…
Afterwards, in the evening, the distant
limestone cliffs are fleshed with
sunshine, lustrous with life's image.
The cry becomes a song. A rhapsody.
You can hear it now, tingling
just beneath the scalp. You realise
this music was before your birth.
You watch the dolphins roll the waves
over, turning the ocean inside out.

John Allison

I search the faces in the cars
at the place
where our roads home cross
as if our lives
might ever intersect again.

Bill Tibben

Space Travel
Li Bai

We part, and go our separate ways,
a lasting compact made to travel unperturbed
till our next tryst, upon a distant smudge
far out into the Milky Way.

Fragment translated from the Chinese
by *Rene Manning*

A prayer in the temple of Venus

(After Horace, III: 26)

I satisfied the girls
well enough until recently,

served, not without military honour;
now my ram, my weapon,

rod for prying doors,
flashlight wandering at midnight,

worn-out songs of the 60s, strummed
on my warped guitar,

are hung on the left wall of this temple
consecrated to my Goddess,

whose Mother is the Sea.
But, dear Goddess, queen,

who liveth and reigneth on Cyprus,
at Memphis, far from winter's

blistering sting, grant me, at the last,
this favour:

raise your whip and gently lash
the heart of unyielding Ellen.

Richard Deutch

Sound of Waiting

I am waiting for you to come back.
Lying on this beach, stranded,
with one eye blinking,
I feel myself pressed
into the shells and pebbles of this rough shore.

I am waiting for you to come back.
All I hear is the constant sea waves,
the overcast skies mourn the lost day,
cream foam spews across the sea,
and the sleet of rain is fine and cold.

I am waiting for you to come back.
There is no song out there,
only the gull screams
whipped by the hollow wind.
Rescuers arrive in yellow plastic coats,

they mean well, covering me in water,
digging round my sides, pulling me to the sea,
crying like children,
but I am waiting.
I am waiting for you to come back.

John Weerden

dragon's breath

"then I must know that still
I am in the hands of the unknown God,
he is breaking me down to his own oblivion
to send me forth on a new morning, a new man."

D.H.Lawrence
'Shadows', Selected Poems

"Perhaps all the dragons in our lives are princesses who are only waiting to see us act, just once, with beauty and courage. Perhaps everything that frighten us is, in its deepest essence, something helpless that wants our love."

Rainer Maria Rilke
'Letters to a Young Poet'

Scar

1
Beside water
light is fooled…
baffled down to a confused, sleep collation of tone.
Sandstone verges rub shoulders like adoring grandparents –
croon over the newborn each-moment
of this clear pool drinking itself.

Beside water
a thin argument of smoke has the eucalypts
strung taut – agitated. He gathers enough
for a cup of tea in an old can/ "Farmland Creamed Corn"
then sets the billy to work.

The sunglasses were a *gift*.
Good luck left them in someone's bag at Bondi Beach
right beside the wallet.
And now a lens falls out startling him
as unfiltered light invades the sleep-hungry eye.
Another fucken hassle.

The national park, a public track
but not too bad 'cept
weekends, school holidays.

If anyone could get an answer
it would be that he was waiting.

With an appointment

The rosellas are mocking. Brown snakes
are rolling in the aisles
through days as poor

as a lost string of rollie tobacco.

This busy, empty green parcel
beneath a ridge line of nice sewered homes.
For six months a bastard climb
for batteries, beer, cans. Milk.

Autoteller answering back
each pension fortnight

Occasional unattended property,
a brick and the grab.

Then long rainy nights
cold in a cupped hand cave.
Radio muttering only to him.

2
The 10-year-old boy
came here regularly with his friends.
Ugly but cunt is cunt
and *Fat Boy* is here alone today, asking for a match.
He wants to build a nice little fire
just like the man.

They sit on opposing shelves of rock.
The boy is feeling the warmth, the importance
of his private conflagration.
The man slips off into the green
and even the gods are surprised
at what happens next.
An interruption, so random that the lizards
almost miss the history, scribbling notes
from the fork of a tree.

3
Fish are feeding,
an unhealthy, hyperactive swarm of insect wings
disturb the whispers of the stream.
A ringtail is crying in her sleep
above a slash of early spring flowers.

The bush is unfazed,
her processes orderly and complete.
Given time, all his trash
will be buried or reborn.
The man has gone
to the next scarred diary page

beside water.

Les Wicks

Note on 'Scar'

I wrote a poem that began *Beside water*. It was a thank-you for the healing sustenance bodies of water have always provided. A couple of weeks later I was bushwalking and came upon a tableau very similar to the one described in **Scar**. It drove home to me how there are always multiple realities underway in any given moment.

The use of the word *cunt* is central to the picture of the protagonist in this poem. Nowadays the word, when used by men (primarily against women), is the most extreme term available to express both dismissal and hatred. Few words are so charged.

The extremity of its current usage means that men fairly rarely use it because it says more about the speaker than it does the subject.

It is from his position of extremis that the protagonist reduces and dismisses the boy by use of this word.* Using it again, he then reduces all sexual release to that same bleak zone of alienation and repugnance. By implication, as a party to this sexual release, he further denies his own self-worth. Here is an individual removed from all those fundamental human needs... association, affiliation and intimacy.

What happens? The very randomness of the protagonist's life means a range of outcomes could occur. Maybe an arriving bushwalker will disrupt the afternoon's looming catastrophe. Either way the bush, the water doesn't care: it is we humans who shape consequence around it. We drink from the same source. As always with us complicated apes, the sustenance varies wildly.

Les Wicks
(*As in original version of poem. This version has compressed two lines into one. *Ed.*)

"I must practise silence."
Sumie Goto

Wind, be strong enough to erase
all trace of my everyday errors.

Mario Licon Cabrera

The Watch

Unlike Gethsemane,
it rains. Unlike Gethsemane,
none sleeps. Fifty pairs of eyes watch
as candles glow and souls intone
the words you spoke –
bread into body,
wine into blood,
gifts cast beyond deserts, rich
symbols across a needing earth.
I kneel. I watch bread
being broken, to share
in your name. Yet your wisdom,
that night, not seating one
of my kind among your twelve
at supper, not having one
who might speak for these fifty
and me in our mad meekness,
escapes me.

For if one, for modest measure,
had been at your table, she might
have washed the feet of the poor,
of the weary, the worldly,
tonight in your name.
Yet we remain the unwashed,
forever the unclean.
Never, forgive me,
your dancer. Never
your symbol playing servant
at the altar. Never the actor.
Always the prop. Never
one of the few, your chosen
few; we are destined in this ritual
to be shadows in your divine human
play. And this pattern we dance
along steps, along walls, pining

in pews, in penance, never,
forgive me, open armed at your altar.

Did you, I wonder
mean it to be two,
please spare us three, thousand
annual performances of such
public rejection?
Is this your advance
from the desert for my sisters?
From being whores, it is said
at the centre
of temples? Prided, paraded, mere
costumed whores who might comfort
or confront as men came needing?
Is this all God offers?
a choice between whoredom
and meekness, depending
which desert she springs from?
I kneel. I pray. I weep.
I rage and resolve
to stay away.
Yet, I watch,
awake.
Unlike Gethsemane.

Joanna Millicer Hempel

Vision

"I smash the mirror to see you."

Shawki Moslemani
Translated from the Arabic **Where the Wolf is**
by *Noel Abdulahad* and *Raghid Nahhas*

child's play

blue-yellow flames flicker
in the gas heater
I stand to one side
still feel cold
no matter how close I am

the flickering draws me closer
I feed the hem of my dress
into the yellow
watch it catch alight

I've done it before
lots of time
brushed flames away
with my hands

this time it doesn't work
I can't put them out
flames run up
the front of my dress

Mummy runs in
she shouts at me
with her beer-cold voice
makes rough movements
over my dress
I stagger like she does
when Daddy hits her

Mummy belts the flames out
with her hands
I shiver

Felicity Daphné Baldry

Untold Letter

You are like a reluctant *nenuphar*
Refusing to let your petals bow.
You want to be part of the landscape
You inhabit. What is it within you
That rejects the one of your forefathers?

Your heart misses the richness
Of their dreams that made you.
You reject the safety-board
Of tradition born in a hemisphere
Whose cultures you feel alien to.
It sucks people out of their depth
To resist where they originate from.

Your persona enflamed, raged
At my sense of belonging.
My painful conclusions
Not a cry for pity but for inclusion.
As a prayer for those who perished,
The edge my family walked along, aleatory,
As a panic that lasted so many years.

Your nascent liberation,
A sacrifice your blood does not demand.
Indelible embryo, I can explain.
You were fed comfortable alleluias
By those whose bones
Will feed this arid soil.

Your soul needs food of nature more complex.
In your blood run goblets of mine,
Its streams of sanitized stories
Your ears accepted eagerly.

Your spirit house longs for
Jettisoned limitations.
Like sleep overpowered by your own fragrance,
You blossom with the balm of your mother,
The problematic but true resin of your father
And, of course, with your own sweet savours
Disseminated all around you.

The incense stick, to smell of frangipani
Has to burn the dipped charcoal
Gathered by destitutes,
Or was it by the innocent hands
Of hungry children who do indeed often smile?

Irina Spinadel

Stone

Oh!
How in your eyes
all became stone!

Shawki Moslemani
Translated from the Arabic **Papers of Solitude**
by *Raghid Nahhas* and *Noel Abdulahad*

Family

But for the family,
The child inside each person, would survive.
For cruelly soon, is he enclosed,
By society's inescapable architecture.
From an astonished heavenly body
It's senses unrestrained
Relentlessly, is he fashioned
Into a heartbeat in traction,
Responding to the only proof of its existence
This disparate collection of creatures can accept.
The same, self-important confusion,
Mothers and fathers, from the cave to the brownstone,
Have honed to a superbly didactic rhythm,
For fear of being unjustified,
For fear of being alone,
For its branches to carry forth,
Christ's cross of hope and suffering.

Danny Gardner

"I love you and I am afraid."
Man to Woman in Blackwattle Bay Park, Glebe

"The darkness is digesting me."
Danu Huan Ho

"All we possess becomes our debt."
Christopher Bodame

English

In the beginning it was English.
In English we are born and named.
No language has ever been or ever will be like English.
English has power and prestige, experience and wealth.
English created our wide brown land for English, of English, by English just as God greated English.
English is the universal language.
Eucalyptus is an English tree. Kangaroo is an English beast.
Wombat is an English marsupial. Waratah is an English flower.
Womerah is an English stick.
They live in the Oxford English dictionary.
Trees bloom in English, cities thrive in English, countries are named in English, cars are restored in English, cows are slaughtered in English.
English is the only language. Every other language is foreign, spoken by foreigners.
Those who speak, see or think in any other language must understand the error of their ways before they besmirch the sanctity of English values which we continue to uphold as true and bountiful for a land born, bred, named, trained and loved in English.
We write laws in English. We brew beer in English. We create gardens in English. We mould landscapes in English. We irrigate rivers in English. We civilize natives in English. We flood valleys in English.
We heal the sick in English. We receive Nobel prizes in English. We bury the dead in English. We fight fire in English. We enjoy the weather in English. We vanquish the wilderness in English. We feel pain in English. We feel compassion in English.
Every fibre in our bodies hums in English.
The sun rises in English.
Daily affairs are conducted in English. English conductors conduct English classes in English.

We comb our hair in English. The moon is filled with English. The dingoes howl in English. We go to war in English. We defeat our enemies in English. We congratulate ourselves in English. We maintain our suspicions in English. We build walls in English. The sun sets in English.
Does not the asylum seeker reject himself in English! The black man humiliates himself in English! Does not the refugee incriminate himself in English? Do we not wash our hands in English?
English is a rabbit rushing down its burrow on the riverbank where it breeds and overpopulates and ravages the interior of the hinterland like a rogue conversation.
English is a shell we pick from the beach and hold to our ear to listen to English. English lives on the ocean in a ship under full steam. Seabirds glide past looking for leftovers of English. An unknown island appears on the horizon. The captain gives his orders to change course in English. The hull of the ship makes contact with unidentified foreign objects beneath the English surface of the water. Rocks pierce the metal skin of the English hull and the ship sinks in English. Hundreds of lives are lost in freezing English. A few hundred more are saved in English and the waves speak to us in English.

Ray Wittenberg

...and the storyteller does not know
when he himself becomes the story, and how!
Shawki Moslemani
Translated from the Arabic **Where the Wolf Is**
by Noel Abdulahad and Raghid Nahhas

Fruit of the Elephant
(A Carving in the Art Gallery of New South Wales)

The poacher
stalks
his prey
downwind,
takes aim with his gun
and the ground shudders
as the elephant falls.

Later
The artist
creates
a masterpiece:
a mandarin
carved
from the tusk of the elephant.
Apricot tinted skin
cream segments of flesh:
a New Year's gift
for a Chinese emperor.

Hilarie Lindsay

"Fool, victory does not confirm your rightness."
Jacques Goldman

"History isn't what it used to be."
Michael Sharkey

"A one-sided person tends to travel in circles."
Christopher Bodame

Contrast the Aboriginal vision with the British tradition which (reconciliation or not) is the social and political matrix which governs the way Australians interact with the land, the plants and the animals of Australia.

The Aboriginal tradition? A dreaming interaction between spiritual beings and people - each aware of the other and keeping a spiritual, ecological harmony between the land, people and animals.

The British tradition was, and still is, extractive - designed to take from Australia and send to the "Home Country" whatever could be mined, farmed or killed. We live so deeply on this British tradition that it weaves a spell over us making us unable to focus on its exploitative premises.

Steven Guth

Hello, I am a child.
I love to play and listen to stories,
  to feel the wind and smell the trees,
  to wonder at the moon...
Why doesn't the moon fall down?

Hello, I am a child.
I love to hear the kookaburras laugh,
  to swim in the billabong,
  to climb gum trees and red hills,
  to watch the yellow sun across the sky.
Why are my aunt and uncle and my cousin
  sniffing petrol?

Hello, I am a child.
I love to see all the birds fly up and
run along the lake shore,
  to help with my father's cattle,
  to cook with my mother in the grass house.
Why are all the people dying?

Hello, I am a child.
I love to skip and run,
  to dance in the hot sun,
  to slide down the sandhills,
  to watch swaying camels go by.
Why did a bomb kill my mother,
my sister and my brother?

Hello, I am a child...

Jacques Goldman

Out of the city it was as if the fighting
Was not happening had never happened;
We had our separate peace there
That summer and all the summers
Of the war, only odd clues
From Saturday movies – a leading man
Unaccountably uniformed,
Chocolate gone, a street dug up.

Once on film, in black and white
Rows of faces of a captured march
Exhausted, relieved by their defeat;
Suddenly in the camera pan, a face
Which stopped it, pulled it close to such
Surprising beauty in that place.

Robert Gurry-Zentner

"A half truth is a homeopathic portion of a lie."
Christopher Bodame

"Bravery wins a lost fight."
Christopher Bodame

End of Form

Grey mid-day
Toll of school bell,
Poppy in the minefield,
A war-child's war-child legacy.
Echoes mocking in a quadrangle game,
The left-last-year
Now forever-unemployed,
Become council flat gangs,
Terrorists' apprentices:
The joke that kills,
Nuclear mutants; the feeling before the fact.

You've all seen the bollocks,
Now it's the clash of the specials.
But how could these rut-runners be a nation's children?
And for whom then, do these sirens sing?
Poverty's factory animals
Bums bare against the barbed wire?

Blood leaves an indelible graffiti:
History class
Is in these rioting streets
Today.

Danny Gardner

That night when all the stars cried
and God chose you to be His guest,
I understood the darkness of night
I understood and I saw my soul fly away
I saw my soul leave.

Assad Cina

An old war

We'll send the boys and girls to war.
There are weapons of mass destruction
And they'll be the first to know.
It's our duty to bush and country,
It's our duty as elder statesmen
To make this sacrifice, to make amends,
And to keep our world safe.

Margaret Smith

(After Blake)

A Mozambique baby
drinking brown water
scrambles eternity.

Ten Ch'in Ü

Where the Wolf is

My bird too has not returned
from its journey.

Silently I search for a star that
once beamed, and vanished.

I witnessed
the slaughter of the butterflies,
quivering muddy dreams in strange lanes,
ants pushing carriages and
the night watchmen running away with the cargo.
Recklessly I mend the holes.

The one obsessed by the passion of the sun
is my comrade.
The crippled hungry tiger
is my comrade.
Those injected with forgetfulness
are my comrades.

And the desert is mine.

The green rain is pouring
over the slopes where
the wolf awaits
a bird that has not returned.
I come out of the dust
and pull along my blind men.

Shawki Moslemani
Translated from the Arabic by *Noel Abdulahad* and
Raghid Nahhas

Letter to Picasso in Baghdad

Do not send me another Guernica
show me instead the living,
those you have met.
Describe their houses,
the carpet where you sat,
the imprint that you made in its pattern,
the reflection of faces in tableware.

In the spaces left
describe their text,
the way the hand turns,
the rhythm of the potter
as his brushstrokes elongate words
into design.
Describe the concept of beauty
as praise for God.

Describe the call to prayer,
the prayer mat,
the ululations rising in silence.

Describe silence.

Pat Pillai

A Country

It took its name
from water
and started to flow.
The foam we saw
riding the waves
was its people.
The grass over the dunes
their ribs.

A country
whose men all
had departed, and so
the women were wed
to trees.

Wadih Sa'adeh
Translated from the Arabic by *Sargon Boulus*

"If I was not there, how could I tell you about it?"
Anis Ghanem

Gunê:
And now only me. Now you must remain silent. And I'll be saying words that I know by heart. I can't alter a single sound. Even the pattern of breathing is imposed upon me...and all the forthcoming phrases will be methodically deceiving my feelings. It may offend you. I am allowed to feel my own feeling, but without altering any sounds, vowels, consonants...So how am I to express myself if everything I say may contradict what I feel? Will you be able to detect my truth that is hiding like a little girl behind this water of words? These words which are assembled by someone who doesn't even know about my existence. So, I probably will be telling you stories, which are irrelevant, which are not mine though they all act as if they represent me...Now I have to dress you up, for instance, in this magnetically purified piece of fabric just to protect your body and your mood. It has been precisely described...the entire ritual has been encoded in me... it's not written down or recorded...I just know the procedure, not even knowing why I know it...or where I know it from. And you are not able to detect whether what I am telling you right now is what I know or not...though you know the background of this speech...and you know that these words are not mine...so maybe I don't know all the rituals...or maybe, coincidentally, I know them all perfectly well...These words are really difficult to remember. They seem to be inconsistent and often illogical, but I remember them all...simply because I don't know how not to remember them. It prevents me from remembering other things, like... well, I don't remember other things. But maybe I remember other things and this speech disallows me to talk about other things...these words are depriving me of me. Yes. And you see, these words themselves admit their own cruelty. So it may be that they will torment you...they'll tease you or play dirty tricks on you...and on me as well, since they are not mine...so I am becoming a tormentor...though I'm not...because I don't agree

with them...I disagree with almost all of them...but even these words I may agree with are not mine either...some of them can please you...or even give you a breath of life and hope...and I'd like to use them, to pronounce them in such a way that you'd be content, or at least enriched...or maybe just happy, enlighten... and I am forced to address them to you right now...but, still they aren't mine. I was already forced to claim their equivocation, you see. How can you believe me now that I love you more than I have ever loved anything, that I can't live without your presence, your sight, your touch and your voice...how can you believe me if you already know that all these words have been forced upon me...it is possible that they by chance do match me...but how are you to know that? How can you trust me? It is also possible that you may, for your own convenience and your own pleasure, trust *them* more than you'd ever trust *me*, and than what? What would become of me? And if you decide to choose *them* rather than *me*, I wish I'll be able to refute their meaning...only because they are not mine...even despite the fact that some of them possibly represent what I feel. But I can't do that because they also serve the other purpose. They shall heal wounds, even wounds that have not yet been inflicted...so you must trust them, although they will never tell you more than you already know...they'll never provide you with a revelation or with new news. They'll steer you through a labyrinth of your own animation and will evaporate with you mimicking the final adjective. They will assist you in formatting your own beliefs and your doubts, they will guide your love, your hate; they'll even exacerbate your imagination and will deny all your possible reveries. They will make you a liar, even if you endeavour to contradict their assertion. You have no choice. You must trust them, for you are not provided with any other means of perception. Words can desert you, and when they do you'll expire. Even when you are numb or deaf you are still beleaguered by words. You are beleaguered by them so long as you perceive their sound or imagine their silhouettes. And what do they do to me right now? They leave things unfinished...

incomplete. They disallow me to work out what they are for. They make me practical, sober...They delineate my memory and force me to rely solely on them. I am forced to remember only what's in them. Even if I remember beyond them they won't grant me permission to go beyond them. But maybe I remember other things; your smile, the warmth of my tears, my pain...but this memory, or rather its pronunciation, belongs to words not to me. They don't match the situation... A list of things to do: touch your forehead. Do it while saying the following sentence. This is the end of the sentence. Say the following sentence without doing anything. Touch your lips... gently...softly. Now conclude the sentence with a deep sigh. Now I must say that I don't remember what I've been talking about. Obviously you won't believe me, but maybe these words are prearranged for this very purpose. You mustn't trust *me*. Never. Whatever I do or say is aimed at destroying you, because I despise you...I never loved you, I was never comfortable with your presence...but I was forced to say that I loved you, so I had to act as if I really did. And this declaration is not supported by the assurance that these words aren't mine. They are mine and they are truthful. And I enjoy telling you all this because now I have courage...I want you to know that I can't stand your presence...your very being disgusts me...it appalls me...and I wish that you've never existed, that the very idea of you had never been invented...and that I will never be near you...I'd rather die than allow myself to be admired by your oppressive selfishness...and remember that from now on, even when I am forced by the rules or situation to be kind to you, it will always be false...because deeply inside me there is a profound discomfort, an enormous hate and abhorrence to you. I can say it all safely now since you are not permitted to produce even the slightest sound, since you are forced by circumstances to just hear me. And even if these words aren't mine...even if I'm forced to wear their shapes...even if I, at this very moment, really think and feel something completely opposite, these words will hang between us forever and ever... and we will never allow ourselves to ignore their matter. We will always be haunted by their subsistence. It is almost the end of my strictly structured way of talking. Yes. This is the end of it. Now.

(fragment)

Bogdan Koca

Journeys

"All journeys are return journeys."
Paul Theroux

We arrived in Bendigo
towards the end of summer
right on up to the end of the road
and the end of love—
we walked among the ruins
looking for the signs.

Beside the gutted hut
a corrugated iron water-tank
involved in its own autumn
shed its rusted leaves, exfoliations
of another time.

A rusty hinge
hung off the door jamb, letting
any wind decide
and everything go by:
in / out   in / out   in / out

You said it then, and turned
away into its truth—
journeys, yes, they always do that
don't they, throw us back
upon ourselves, every destination
telling us exactly
where we're coming from.

John Allison

Drought

Wind dances with dust
the rain god shuts its umbrella
a wheat stalk withers.

Hilarie Lindsay

Moment in Time

The line of time thrusts forward
at unimaginable speed,
straight and true, relentless,
unable to be diverted,
overriding everything in its uncaring
silent velocity
until you punched a hole in it
and time sagged, breathless, astonished by the
sheer shock of the blow.
Now, looking back,
all I see is a shooting blind white trail,
straight and uncaring.

John Weerden

In the tunnel, in the bone

Soon time will end.
Winds are approaching the immense wall.
And there they will buckle under.
They passed quickly, and the race is over.
Finally the winds will rest.
Time cracked open. It hangs only from one stitch.
I await its decline, its resounding fall to earth.

Life begins on the last day.
Days are many, but life is meagre.
It is delayed from day to day. And when there's only one day left, it rushes into it with its entirety hoping to live there...in this way life begins, just when it's ending. That's why life will never be lived!

I've still one day left, what should I do?

Begin life? With what will I begin this life?
With whom? How? With what action or speech?

And if I happen to meet someone, what will I say to him? With you, now, I will begin my life? And if I said this, and he responded, how will I live a life I'm saying goodbye to? How will I live the death of life?

I woke up very early. Those who will depart must wake up very early to enhance their final days. They must witness the dawn, at least, before they go.

In this room's space exist the splinters of humans who lived thousands of years ago, whom I say goodbye to, and become splinters like them.
I say goodbye to the pulse of planets that reaches me across the vacuum of space from distant galaxies.
The galactic swishings, the dust of stars, the air born

a million years ago crossing silently an immense space in order to reach me.
I say farewell to gasping volcanoes, to the drizzle of faraway swamps, to the pictures, the chairs, the mirrors, the clocks, my children's eyes, their shoes scattered carelessly on the floor. I say goodbye to the waves that penetrate my body, to the vibrations that come from the oldest place, the big bang!

Did I have to clash with myself all this time, and everything else with me, in order to become a silent prey in the end? Wasn't I able, a long time ago, to relieve this noisy world of one voice at least?

The universe must rest. Voices must all become silent.

Oh, for some quiet!

I can't describe the day, I can't describe anything. Speaking is nothing but betrayal. They don't speak on the last day. They just shut up and leave.

Those hills were silent also. And we were, with the stirring of sun and wind, the only sound.

But we, with that monotonous movement in the stillness of death, had snared mysteries from the bones.

How were we, simple as we are, flung between the jaws of immensities, to invent places that would protect us? How were we able to continue until today! We were no mortals. But certain bones of cattle and dry sticks saved our lives. It wasn't life that protected us, but death.

We mixed our births with grass. And under those thin
ears of wheat our land found a shade. We never wore
clothes, or trinkets or bracelets. But our breath was
our cloth and ornament. We were naked. We found
warmth in the firewood born of our panting,
which was dry, and so ignitable.

Under the reign of flame, we had many celebrations
for which we selected many guest seats, within our
pores. Life was within our skin, not outside. Thus,
we lived life in its secret hideout, in dimness, in the womb,
before it was born.

Our celebrations were tended in our veins, not in
public squares. Our habitation in the imagination of
place. Our caravans in the head, not on the roads...

We lived the anti-birth: there was our childhood, our
youth and old age. And we met life once, before the
door of death.

During the war, my father looked for a bone in the
wilderness to crush it with a stone and satisfy his hunger.
From those crushed bones a number of
children were born, among whom I was one. I was the
son of a crushed bone.

Inside the bone a tunnel opens now, where there is a
wilderness and annals, and where my father is
walking again.

He walks, taking me with him, hand in hand, looking
for a bone.

We walk in the heart of the bone, looking for it. When
we saw it at last, we were already far away.

We had become two bones, in which there was a tunnel where people walked around looking for bones.

I walked in the bone tunnel. My father had put me at the invisible point in the folds, in the dusty emptiness, the primal mother of the life of bones.

I turn my head back now and look: to those lost in bone marrow, to the ones who stand on its pavements, to those who stretch out their hands seeking an exit, to the dead with the electricity of spirit, to those who look for a stone to crush their bone and eat it, to the ones who have just entered, and scarcely know what they are doing.

I turn my head back and look: when I cast the marrow out, I had opened my passage. Emptiness was the way. Emptiness was the stone.

My child sleeps close to me. I will not say goodbye to her. I shall go to death as if I were going out to bring her some candy. I shall go to death as if going to a shop.

I was a little boy when my father carried me in his arms to a shop. He entered and said: This is my son, give him some candy. All throughout that day, I played with a handful of sweets.

But why do I reminisce over my childhood like someone entering life when I'm actually leaving it? And what's the use of recalling it when there is no room even for a phantom? Whole populaces, even those that are extinct, still reside here. I stare out of the window hoping they would walk on my glance, and get out. This room's arteries must rest!

Those who got out, left their splintered eyes on the walls. Those who stay, hang up the sheep of their breath and ate...I'll be the one to walk on my glance through the window, and disappear.

Those days, which are gone now, were not more than practice for entering life. Life is a mere practice for entering it. But it ends there, and we never enter. What we live of life is that practice. We live only the pre-birth. In the arteries that are still unformed. In the featureless face. Inside the entrails' ethereal darkness. We live on the edge, between being and nothingness. At the door. And when we attempt to exit, we are shattered, like a heavenly body, in the abyss.

So I'm not speaking about a life. I'm not describing a birth, but its absence. I'm not writing about a light, but a darkness. Not remembering what was, but what was supposed to be...This supposition that may finally be what we call our life.

...And saying farewell to it, perhaps, the only certainty. A few more seconds and I shall have my first certainty!

I will celebrate my veins. I will welcome those who emerge suddenly from the void, and dance with them.

Then I'll go back to the bone. To my father's secret. To the tunnel. Cast aside the guts, smile and go on my way.

Wadih Sa'adeh
Translated from the Arabic by *Sargon Boulus*

Some Thoughts on Love

1
We see it clearly
only when we look slightly away from it,
otherwise it is too dazzling to analyse.
But we are human.
We know analysis is over-rated!

2
We must trust our responses for what they are,
And admit, if it goes wrong:
my perceptions are my own fault.
And there are so many kinds of love,
and sometimes one kind can turn into another.
They all form a fabric we alone cannot complete
Even if it is only in company with another presence
That may be able to answer our night prayers:
To trust in what we cannot control.

3
It's too easy to be tender and not true.
I'm in search of a grace,
But in poetry, I approach beauty via its opposite.
To speak of it would be the first part of its destruction.
Only by indulging in the comedies and the horrors,
Life's other pervasive realities,
only by laying hands upon the dragon's breath,
only by dressing myself first, in the mane of the beast,
can I approach the surrender of the heart.

4
"I love you," he said.
"They all say that," she said.
"Don't you trust me?" he asked.
"Can't you tell me how much, you love me?" she replied.

5
There are many kinds of love.
But, one to one,
We feel it before we know it, or understand.
It's an ideal we hope we can bring to the everyday.
Its power to make us happy, could, surely, save the world.
Yet, we mark its presence more by its effects.
Only when life's flow falters
do we see our incompleteness,
fear that we have never loved, or been loved.
The more we seek it then,
The less it seems to be found.
It can only be granted by non-expectations,
And, in our fortune, or otherwise,
We each give it one more guise in the game:
the world can still be saved by our tomorrow.
Otherwise its fragility,
Our strangeness to our fellows
Would crush us.

Danny Gardner

Coal

Because he has only little bread
they burdened his face with weariness
and because he loves the sun and the trees
he was hanged upside down

Shawki Moslemani
Translated from the Arabic **Papers of Solitude,**
by *Raghid Nahhas* and *Noel Abdulahad*

A God of Small Things

It's years since he was inside a church
and nothing's changed. Not the echo of his feet
not the water in the stoup or the dusty light.
Not the incense stinging his throat
nor candles flickering in the gloom
guilt hidden in the shadows.
Forever, young boys in spotless smocks,
heads bowed in the quiet
longing for the sun and surf,
their boards propped waiting at the door.
Forever, saints immortalised in stone
gazed down upon his mother where she knelt.
Throughout the years
not one responded to her prayers,
reduced the violence or the pain.
And now her coffin at the altar,
the music ripping up a tide
curling like the angel wings of waves.

Paula McKay

Mexico City

On the worst days, the sky is white
We cannot walk
We drive three million cars

Jacqueline Buswell

I, Kevin Cyborg

Once out of nature I shall never take
My bodily form from any natural thing

W.B. Yeats in 'Sailing to Byzantium'

"Will we evolve into a cyborg community? Linking people via chip implants to superintelligent machines seems a natural progression - creating, in effect, superhumans... We will still fall back on speech in order to communicate with our newborns, however, since it will take a few years before they can safely get implants of their own, but in the future, speech will be what baby talk is today."

Prof. Kevin Warwick

In August 1998, Professor Kevin Warwick of the Department of Cybernetics at the University of Reading had a silicon chip transponder implanted in his forearm which allowed him to communicate with a computer programmed to respond to his actions. On 14th March 2002 a one-hundred-electrode array was surgically implanted into the median nerve fibres of his left arm enabling him to control an electric wheelchair and an intelligent artificial hand. In addition to being able to measure the nerve signals transmitted down Professor Warwick's left arm, the implant was also able to create artificial sensation by stimulating individual electrodes within the array. This was demonstrated with the aid of Kevin's wife Irena and a second, less complex implant connecting to her nervous system. Phrases in italics are the professor's own, or closely based on them.

Greetings Flesh-Forms, you sad Meat Puppets!
Hail hydro-carbon-copied douche-bag buses
for bacteria, god-knows-what permutations of shit!

"Be afraid, be very afraid." The future's here
and neither the meek nor these shy off-cuts of meat
shall inherit this earth of transcendent joy and fear.

I was born human (in, and of, itself, no great disgrace)
- *though this was clearly an accident of fate,*
a condition merely of time and place.

Something to be overcome,
like a weak head for love or alcohol,
(but I digress) - I've come, oh baby, I've come

a long way since those first head-bangingly alarmed
security-coded doors swung so freely open,
mainlined to that connection spiked into my arm.

Get high, get laid, and now each rush is saved to disk.
Each moment doubly savoured, so nice I lived it twice.
Carpe diem takes on a whole new dimension.

Soon there will be sensational libraries on-line.
Imagine! my greatest moments racked like vintages.
Taste my life like fine, fine wine.

Proust's gone educational. (To sophisticate your own response, you
may choose my ***Special Connoisseur's Memory Palate*** ©.
Think downloadable *déjà bu*.)

This new chip taps into your nerve fibres;
through scanning neural spike events
you'll explore a whole new range of sense.

An aid to new philosophy (*When supra-threshold events occur,*
the signal window surrounding the event is
time-stamped, stored for off-line analysis.)

But for now, imagine your all-time favourite
orgasms logged - your *Greatest Hits.*
His-'n'-hers implants mean you'll really sing the body electric.

Kisses blown across Atlantics or Pacifics.
A *whole new world* of telepathic sex
is your oyster, caresses texted

like Don Juan's back-catalogue. Unloaded down her spine,
new plug-ins - sensual attachments -
touch-typed fast as emailed Valentines.

Your are the resurrection and her life.
Imagine - *Your significant other jacked right into your limbic system.*
Now she is truly your other half, your one true wife.

No longer any impediment to the marriage of true minds.
You meld and it's thought to thought.
Leave all doubt behind.

You need only think, to twitch her with a blink.
No need to ask if she comes.
You speak her body language. You are no longer dumb.

To continue bloodless, forever pure information,
wholly ghost in your, or her, machine.
Your cells will age, but cyberdrugs will cure cancer, relieve
depression.

Alternative pathways will help the blind to see, the deaf to hear.
The miraculous will be commonplace.
I leave that to the medicine men. Us visionaries hurry on.

Outside it's the 21st Century and once again it's getting dark.
The priests are gathering like crows.
It's time to chose: they think the body is a temple.
I give you the World's Greatest Amusement Park.

Cliff Forshaw

dolly the sheep

cloned dolly created the next age
and several years of media gold
lived ordinary   by all accounts
walked   ate   ruminated   shat
then she began to rapidly grow old
like some kind of bovid dorian gray
with time not on her side and fate pushed too far
like a burnt out rock star she did not fade away

she looked just like mick jagger's neck
(shimmying shoulder under the royal sword)
staggering benighted towards posterity
dolly died for the greater good   or was it evil
a voice replies   who else wants to mess with me
have some sympathy for the devil

Bill Tibben

Do not say you are only human
for I know you're not man-made.

Christopher Bodame

Second Time Around

Have you ever noticed that there are events in your life that are so singular, so out of the ordinary, that you either have to isolate them to put them away into a box so they can be ignored, or acknowledge and accept them even if you do not understand them, in which case they radiate out and fill your whole life, illuminating both the past and the future? Maybe one of these events has happened to you, and you have tried to put it in a box. If you succeed, life probably seemed easy. You could carry on as if nothing had happened. Oh yes, there was *that*, but it really did not have any significance, and there certainly were no lasting effects.

Putting them in a box is certainly the safer way of dealing with such events, for if we let the extraordinary get a hold on us there is no telling where it will lead. It starts out innocently enough, like setting foot on some little used path that runs by our backdoor. We think we will just follow it down to the corner store to pick up some milk and cookies but it does not let us go. It sweeps us away to ever larger and larger thoroughfares, to undreamed-of adventures. We become human flotsam dragged away by the current and the majesty of life.

I think that this is the difference between saints and the rest of us. The saint, when confronted with the undeniable presence of God says "*Yes*! Oh *yes*! Please, *more*, oh give me *more*!" They do not fear drowning. The rest of us, in our small lives, when confronted with the ever-present reality of the Divine, say "Huh? I wonder what that was? Could it have been real, do you think?" And we build a box of dark and solid wood to contain that which we have made ordinary. But I have found that no matter how dark and strong these boxes, the miraculous will out eventually. And when it does, that path whose existence we have denied for so long will carry us where it will, and we end up where the saint started, saying "*Yes*! Oh *yes*! *Please*!"

This is the story of one of those events.

Once upon a time there was a young man, an ordinary young man, ordinary in every way that matters: middle class, respectable, soon to be well educated; not some King's third son-simpleton who suddenly surprises everyone with his brilliance and wins the day. An ordinary son loved by his mother in ways only a first son can be. As well adjusted as anyone. A youth who loved kites and feared the dark, who played chess and ping-pong, and read and read and read. He finished high school in Europe, college in the States and graduated with a Ph.D. when there were no higher degrees to earn. He moved then, and ended in Jerusalem, that city of gold and war, where he married before returning to the States with his American wife.

It is now late July 1984 and our young man is in Massachusetts attending a weeklong seminar, studying esoteric Christianity and having many conversations. One evening he hears of a memorial service for the victims of the first atomic bomb, and having nothing special to do that night and thinking that this seems like an important event, he decides to attend.

It is a small group that gathers in the classroom under the dining hall. Six or seven, perhaps eight adults, sitting quietly in a circle as the leader explains the Japanese custom of placing candles in small paper boats and setting them adrift to commemorate the victims of Hiroshima. As he listens, and thinks of those candles with their soft light glowing, he begins to cry.

The tears do not start slowly; they are not like some slow drizzle that streaks your windows after a day of lowering clouds. They come quickly in great heaping sobs. Billows of tears that surprise everyone, including himself. And though he knows immediately, intuitively, passionately, why he cries, though this knowledge is present with him before his first tear falls, he can barely believe what he is experiencing. For there is nothing in the leader's description of the candles and boats that prompts his tears. And though he feels the deaths and sorrow surrounding those thousands who died so quickly at the moment of detonation, and even of those who died so slowly later from radiation poisoning, these deaths are not the central fact confronting his spirit and causing his great sobs. What is it then that causes him to close his eyes as if in shame in front of this small group of strangers who have gathered for this evening's commemoration?

It is that with the knowledge of these deaths in his heart, before the eye of his spirit he sees the magnesium-bright flash of detonation, a light brighter than the noonday sun on brilliant sand, a light bright enough to sear his retina, the light beyond light that precedes the mushroom cloud and heralds the death of the atom. And with this timeless flash...no, oh no, not with...within...how can it be within?...identical with this light, now brighter than the sun, there appears a second and yet self-same light, a light that was and is the body of the risen Christ.

Body beyond a body, light that is no light; body of light and spirit itself - and *pain* - oh, how can there be pain in light? Christ's body of light is being torn asunder, rendered down beyond the atoms...again and again destroyed for all the eternity of that timeless moment of detonation. Rendered as completely as the atoms of uranium that gave their existence to feed the fire. Rendered but not overcome! Destroyed, but destroyed to resurrect, not merely as light, but as Life itself! A second resurrection to follow a second death.

He knows that this is why he cries in great heaping sobs. He cries until, not understanding what is happening, someone comes and puts their arms around him, and holds him in his tears.

What would you have done, sitting there on a peaceful Northern evening, among strangers, eyes closed and sobbing, looking into the light and seeing destruction...and Life? Perhaps you would have known to say, "*Yes*, oh please *yes*! *More*, oh please give me *more*!" Perhaps. But perhaps you would have been like our young man, and have said little, only cried and cried, and eventually have said, "There is a meditation. Someone should write this down. Please write this down:

> *Imagine the moment of detonation, before the mushroom cloud forms, when there is only light, majestic and horrible. Then imagine the light, full of love that is the risen Christ. Picture these two side-by-side. Then bring them together, and hold them there, together in that timeless moment of detonation.*

Perhaps then you will then see that we have done something extraordinary...something horrible...something inevitable. Something that we must accept without judgement of ourselves or of those more intimately involved in it than you or I, and must open our spirits to receive as a miracle beyond miracles.

Bruce Kirchoff

Sunflowers, Kosovo

I watched a news report on Kosovo
there were sunflowers
whole fields of them
standing in front of the villages
eyes right   disciplined
ready to lay down their lives

I thought of Vincent in the asylum at St. Rémy
could he have seen this   had a premonition of this war

laying waste to canvas
on a scale not previously witnessed
Vincent fought the vision in his head
the world called that madness
though he lost only one ear
and a lot of paint

Pat Pillai

Arizona War Memorial, Pearl Harbour

Oil seeps from sunken battleships
where drowned sailors keep watch.
I stand on the bow of the *Star of the Pacific.*

As the notes of the *Last Post* drift over the sea,
I hold out my hand to the Japanese man
who stands at my side.

Friends, I say as we shake hands, *no more war.*
I don't understand English, he says
and offers me a piece of chewing gum.

Hilarie Lindsay

covering the distance

Mr Ellis continued "Anne Brooksbank, my partner of 33 years, has told me she is looking forward to the next 33 with love and curses and weariness but I had better henceforth watch it."

Kate McClymont
Sydney Morning Herald 4th May 1999

Weighty Matters

Beginnings come so easily
a first line complete
and beautiful
fills my mind
and I rush for pen and paper
or my keyboard
and having set it down
I know without a doubt
how it will end.

Last lines come so easily
as inevitable as death
always there
challenging me
to justify
an inherent
sense of word.

Titles
often
announce
themselves
obvious
or oblique
but right
and satisfying.

Now middles are another thing entirely. Responsible for deciding if the poem will be short or if the poem will be long, if the space between the first line and the last line will be filled with worth or just a ploy to fill the paper and my time. Middles are important. Middles are a worry. Middles make me think about the diet I'm not on.

Ann Davis

Mixed delights

"Of course," Sumie said,
tucking into the mango and coconut cake
after finishing two of Danu's cinnamon
dribbled with maple syrup pancakes,
"there isn't much point in marrying your
soulmate. What could you possibly learn
from such an easy association, I ask you?
But this is *so* delicious."

Ten Ch'in Ü

Better Than Never

She is there...somewhere,
he said,
not easy to find mind you -
disguised even -
but she is there...to find
if...
and he smiled in that way of his,
if...you never stop looking.
But,
he added quickly,
it doesn't always happen...
only...
maybe...every once in a while.
He thought about that a second,
in truth,
he said,
not really that often,
at best once in a lifetime,

and even then,
there's no guarantee.

When it does,
happen that is,
or rather...if it does,
he stroked his chin and chuckled,
there's that ubiquitous 'if' again.
'If',
he said
has begun to qualify my future.
If it happens...you'll know,
he said,
you will know...when it happens,
because you'll suddenly want
the world to stand still.

So,
here I am,
trying to cram the rest of my life
between an awesome happiness
holding back tomorrow
and the tears of knowing it can't be
done.
There's nothing
I can do
but
exactly like he said,
I know she's there.

David Morris

Snapshot of a Conversation

"Isn't it better never than late?"
Pablo Neruda in **The Book of Questions**

Red party balloons bob in the already garish restaurant
where they have dined on a foreigner friendly menu.
Better to love than hold back
her fortune cookie proclaims in miniscule type.
"Who writes these aphorisms?" she asks.
"Pablo Neruda's mother," he answers inspiredly,
"and afterwards Pablo converts them into questions:
Mama, isn't it better never to hold back than to hold hands?"
They laugh and leave the premises.
"Men are simple," he says as they drive off into the night,
"they want good food...and a cuddle."
A small billboard with a promiscuous promise
I am available day and night nudges the highway.
She asks, "Does a cuddle mean a hug and a kiss or..."
she searches for a suitable term, "something more?"
"Oh, the first," he replies, turning her way
he lowers his eyes into hers,
"leading hopefully to the second."
He grins, then frowns.
"Women are complicated," he narrows on the road.
"They want compliments, understanding,
respect, undivided attention," he sighs.
"Commitment..."
they stop at the lights.
"Sensitivity, your soul - all that stuff,"
he waves a hand in mock despair,
"and then some."
"They want," she says, lifting
herself just a little, "to come..."
She pauses. The lights turn green.
"Into being," she finishes.

Ten Ch'in Ü

Reasoning old landscapes

this arrondissement of Paris is grey   sticks of aerials wire their
irritants
into 17th C roofs   in the crowding out of skies I start to look
for a view
the message lines   the chimney-pots   clash their
incommensurables
I turn direction

the Jewish museum's a building with many floor   records of
periods
the history of being accepted then expelled is registered in notes
on the artefacts
a Torah-crown from Galicia   a model of a synagogue from
Piaski
its wooden interlocking carpentry   as though this is a way to
the present
my walking viewpoint ends in a park   with playing children
flashes of white
swans alternate with water plants
like migratory patches of sun adding warmth to our shoulders
what yields against the past   is that the pain in our throats
comes from trying not to notice what memory can keep
I'd like to wear it down   let it exist only after the way a pearl
forms

Phyllis Perlstone

We dream you alive
(Nightmare for a Dead Sister)

We dream you alive,
you giving advice,
urging on the good
or laughing with your mother
in the light-hearted times we cherished.
You, giggling, as we cross legs for you -
they connect with waste bin:
"Kicked the bucket again!" you chortle,
wicked-grinning as we reach for another wine.

We dream you alive
and you live, your faith,
your wisdom, even your cussedness
as you fight to defy disease,
belittle prognoses,
live long past medical deadlines.

We dream you alive,
remember the fun, the terrible
effort required for life
as normal as possible;
the intellect, the laughter,
even exhausted, youthful tears.

Then one terrible night it changes:
We dream you dead, lost and dead.
We pace, strum, scream frantic, on and on:
you - lost, no one knows where the body lies,
where you are, when, how it happened.
There is no trace, not a thing of you,
no possession, not a single piece of your life.

We had travelled to Greece, we three,
mother, sister, father -left you
in a home - you died -

no one told us, no one cared.
In our real lives we would never have holidayed
without you, never left you out.

We trekked Greek hills pushing wheelchair,
fed you octopus, ouzo, retsina;
ate salads *ochi ladi,* chose our fish to grill,
shared Greek sun, threw you in the sea you loved
...sometimes all four, usually in groups of three:
father, mother, daughter or sister, love, sister...
Translation and laughter marked our stays,
Greek energy, love caring.
"Spastico?" they prayed, hands heavenward,
giving you shells, biscuits,
bringing out chairs to settle and chat,
letting you - a woman - join men in village backgammon.
Your hands not working, we moved your pieces for you.

Never without you, never father, mother, me,
especially not in Greece - no, not in Greece,
our special place. Hunting, then
for Hippocrates' healing spring
in our bid to get you,
given a year to live at 22, well again.

Someone - please- tell us where they put you,
where your smile is, your knowledge,
your cold, hard body at peace.
Never to lose you - never - panic in dream;
never all away without you - panic, desperate,
lonely, searing, screaming panic rises.
But we never found you.

Then it's light and it's morning -
now we have another chance to dream you alive.

Sue Hicks

Second-hand and Antiquarian

One of a few hand-printed
numbered copies signed
by an old-world author whose
later works were said to be ghosted,
I am back in the catalogue, marked
as ‘condition fair’. In a room
at the back of the shop, whose curios
urbanely test the connoisseur’s
sangfroid, is a scruffy
volume with elegant definitions
of ‘good’, ‘near fine’,
and ‘practically mint’. This time
the buyer must judge for herself.
Some foxing on inner pages
never became a resigning matter.

John Miles

Vanajam Kaloo who asked for a blank page in the book.

Man on Robben Island

Seven years in one room
melting
bricks,
bending
bars

With a single, unwavering stare.

Resistance.

Danny Gardner

Burning Books

Words silenced by fire?
Thought is not a caged bird.
Ashes fly in the wind.

Hilarie Lindsay

"Think about it: where does thought come from?"
John Pater

Circles

A man
if he drowses
wakes up
with echoing circles
in his head
and he has children
who want to get out.

A man
worthy of water
is drunk by the sky
until he becomes desert.

A man
becomes
a
m
a
n
blown by the wind.

Shawki Moslemani
Translated from the Arabic **Papers of Solitude**
by *Raghid Nahhas and Noel Abdulahad*

"Can you think a thought that does not exist?"
Christopher Bodame

Australian Artesian Waters

Secret Seas of Life

Welling of waters
Black-veiled river sky
Often in past times
Flowing on by.
Welling of waters
Where have you been?
Under red earth
When the earth had its dream
Coursing a continent
Ocean depth dwells
Watered by vastness
Deep water wells.

Spirit-being of the waters
Blue opal sky
Underground rivers
Flowing on by
Trees whispering spirals
Calling life's rain
Filling earth's thirst dry rivers
Coursing a continent
Life's seas secret dwells
Watering the vastness
Filling deep water wells.

Welling of waters
Azure kingfisher sky
Waters of wellbeing
Soothe all that was dry
The land that was ailing
Is verging on well
Between above and below -
Life's waters all flow -

Rainfall of generosity -
Love's harmony dwells -
Heavenly waters of blessedness
Holy wisdom's deep water wells.

Susan Whitehead
Written for eurhythmy ("speech made visible")

More

The drunkard
is more balanced, more stable

more transparent
in a drunk world.

Shawki Moslemani
Translated from the Arabic **Papers of Solitude**
by *Raghid Nahhas* and *Noel Abdulahad*

Drought
(after Hilarie Lindsay)

Invited to party on
the dying continent,
the rain god took a rain-check.

Ten Ch'in Ü

"The pee is silent as incontinence."
David Pudney

Heavenly Words

The Salvation Army lady said,
" 'Eaven is like the Magic Mile of Motors
on the Parramatta Road, where everyone can trade
'is past in, underneath the patriotic pennants.
Slide your decrepit legs on to the unaccustomed
ground, shuffle three steps along your wheeled dream
with electronic static balancing, powered steering
and eternity of motion, getting nowhere.
For that's the joy of 'eaven – with a haitch."

The grey flannel-suited Mormon said
"Heaven is like a leagues club in the suburbs
where you can loll on motel-turfed
carpets face to face with one-armed deities,
their haloes bright with promise from Christ's
parable of talents, jostling coins and jerking
chrome: jostling, jerking, jostling, jerking,
don't you hear that rhythm and blues?
It's heaven not to hear yourself not thinking."

The soft-spoken Jesuit father said,
"Heaven is like a fast-food franchise selling
hamburgers – with or without –chickens, thick shakes,
apple pies and simulated cream to an omninational
formula. From mountain heights to river flats, seaside
to desert sands, wherever two or three are gathered
together in touring car to savour the world's diversity,
look for the beatific vision of the franchise sign.
For heaven is tasting standard food for ever."

David Tribe

Girl Gone

Girl, gone from me,
out of my arms
girl gone,
all clothes from bedroom, gone,
windows open
perfume, stocking and hangbag vanished,
everything of her, gone
out of my life.
And girl,
peels back the eye of the world.
Her leaps strike shut the clouds.
The city, the roads, the factories,
a vast sheet of newspaper drawn back
before the sudden grin of earth.
And girl runs, laughing,
shedding confetti of newspaper
across the open field.
Girl gone from modern life,
shedding lipstick, hair-mask, face-pak,
shedding nylon, polyester, false fingernail,
peels off eyelash, toe caps, skin-sheer costume,
stepping out of 'they're all lovable' billboards,
shedding hairdryer, radio, diaphragms and dildos,
shedding apron and uniform,
chambermaid's stupid-blonde grin,
shedding waitress slavery, secretary-wife,
dishwashing automaton
shedding surrogate motherdom,
drunkards' nurse nuptials,
shedding office-party prostitution
fate of drug-ring knock-up,
discarding rockstar lay-babydom.
shedding ego of the ornament;

girl sheds bare arms and breasts,
legs, glimpse of clit,
pubic hair;
stripping blank all porno books,
over twenty-one and Cosmo, glossy cover fake,
girl fleeing madness,
running across fields,
gone to find bosom
with goddess, wood-nymph, Venus, angel, Muse, dryad
and all the rest;
laughing and running,
girl on horseback,
girl in the water with the swans,
girl playing with lions and tigers,
girl dressing herself with butterflies;
girl gone from modern life
but for last trap to romantic imagination,
the mirage dream of Eden;
girl sings songs to the sun, now,
kicking all the mirrors of the stars into blackness.

Girl gone from my arms,
everything of her, gone from modern life;
girl was the only innocence
girl is a photograph
girl is a memory
girl said yes to herself
when she died with Marilyn Monroe.

Girl, will you ever be here again?

Danny Gardner

Spring in Suburbia

Mrs Jones looks out her window
at her twelve yellow daffodils.

When she goes outside
she finds that snails have chewed at two.

Her small daughter picks a few
and takes them to her teacher.

A naughty boy with a stick
knocks the heads off the rest.

Out in the cemetery
a few jonquils bloom unseen.

Hilarie Lindsay

The Poem That Escaped

you sit in front of me
you lie in your bed
or maybe you stand in front of the wall
with me stuck onto it
in a less than glorifying fashion
or maybe you have found me in a book
somewhere between pages
or maybe you don't see me at all
and only one of my words catches your attention
and then you stop and you glance at me

I am the poem that escaped

I had enough
I have been used for so many trivial purposes
I've been imprisoned
modified reshaped developed
so many times by an endless gallery of selfish poets
I have been used
transmitting ideas questions and answers
I have been forced to solve the problems of humanity
I have been fixing up unfulfilments
and justifying the deaths of millions
pronouncing love and hatred
denying and praising gods
I have been wearing forms and structures
tailored for me without my own permission
carrying good and bad rhymes and an uncomfortable metre
I've been dismantled and reconstructed freezing on ancient walls
and stinking between old dusty pages
supplying fame and misery hope and predictions
I've been accusing and forgiving
uniting and dividing
loving on behalf of lovers who don't know how to love

I've been crying and laughing
provoking
providing someone's solutions
for any occasion
I've been forced to communicate
all the languages of the world
without my own consent
I've been solemnly recited
for masses
on stadiums
in lavish gardens
by bards
comedians
children with red scarfs over their necks
accompanied by bands
and cannons
I have been in poets' service since my verses
could safely hide their imperfections
I've been deprived of my own voice
to defraud ones lack of imagination

I am the poem that escaped

don't read me out
just look at me
don't distribute me
accept the clumsiness of my freedom
contemplate my solitude
don't tell of me
don't sing me
don't scrutinise me
just let us have an intimate hesitation
a comfortable lack of commitment
let us be silent and thoughtful
with no prejudice with no expectations
don't ever read me out

don't whisper me
using an appropriate diction
correct
clear
round
don't try to heal my wounded vowels
my crooked consonants
and don't betray me by telling poets
of me and you
you are as I am
a poem of silence
you are my kin
for
my existence
my safety
and my wellbeing
is in your eyes
I live without a poet
I can't exist without your sight
your permission
your will
you are in front of me
not knowing
why
what for
I won't provide you with recipes
I cannot answer any of your questions
I wish to celebrate our acquaintance in secret
outliving my eternity
at the bottom of your drawer
between things that matter
memories
old photos
and a long forgotten collection of passion

Bogdan Koca

Wiseman's Ferry

In the days of my obsession
I carried you close to my body:
a sweet totem.

Now we meet, years later;
you, thin as ever,
blue eyes intense in your Renaissance face,
still absorbed in your psychic states
and personal needs;

me, longing to trace
the lines the years have marked,

to be held while you listen to *my* story.

You're still with her
though the daughters have left
and your son has serious problems.

You've been meditating with those monks again
in the bush near Wiseman's Ferry –
going to publish the poems of your years together
then leave her.

You used to say you feared growing old alone –
once said you would come to me.

All right, use me, dear.
I'm still the sponge
that soaks up tears
on the surface of your life.

Wring me out
hang me up to dry:
you can use me another day.

Pip Griffin

Requiem

I do not mean to always come to you,
I do not mean to think every day about you,
when you do not desire it.

I do not mean to gather flowers for you,
I do not mean to live a death without you,
if you do not desire it.

I am driven to this state
by feelings no words can convey.
I am unconscious
until the sight of you awakes me.
You release me from the prison of myself.
You will be ever-young to me
as I am ever-young whenever I am with you.

When you first denied me,
I memorised your loveliness
to make a picture of you
but it faded without the reality to compare.

I brought gifts, and again you denied me.
I pretended you were dead,
but your face kept invading my sleep.

I brought more gifts,
and tried to see you as a friend
but the image of our union, flesh to flesh,
kept pushing my body to touch you.

Can't you see?
It's an impossible situation,
and you must keep your door closed to me now.

You must anger me out of my suffering.
You must evaporate, like an interrupted dream.
And I, must put on
the mask of my non-self.
I must crowd out my life
with detours and indulgent distractions.
I must disclaim all knowledge.
I, must say,
you never existed.

Danny Gardner

I prefer that you scream
but
despite your agony
you are considerate.

Shawki Moslemani
Translated from the Arabic **Papers of Solitude**
by *Raghid Nahhas* and *Noel Abdulahad*

"We are most human when our parallel universes collide and we accept it as logical and, some would say, a predestined meeting."

Danny Gardner

For the Person Who Has Everything

A
great
big
hairy
spider
would
make
a
good
pet
if
you
could
teach
it
to
catch
cock
roaches.
It
could
live
in
the
kitchen
cup
board
be
side
the
heart
at
tack
pills.

Hilarie Lindsay

Leaflet for Lazarus

Please read these notes on leaving kingdom come.
As you have no doubt heard, we did have some
Problems with the Celestial Secrets Act
And its associated fixed term contract,

So your first stop is the debriefing room
Which councils now under updated Doom
Regulations have a duty to provide
for anyone who thinks he may have died.

Once you have Form P45(RD)
And are an Authorised Restitutee,
We send you on a three-day overview
For Life Skills Mentors to empower you

To walk in your protective gear and squeak
And gibber through a hairless working week,
And after that, of course, the choice is yours
(Down the stone steps beyond the double doors).

John Miles

"At least when you talk to yourself, you know someone's listening."

Man speaking into his mobile phone outside restaurants at Crows Nest.

"Today there are no more Mystery centres except those which exist between you and I when we meet. The past, our karmic past, brings us together in the dynamic development of time. What we do at this meeting – that is our freedom of destiny."

Jaap van der Haar

"You can die from loneliness."

Woman on Sydney Tangara train.

"We face many small thresholds every day - a blank page, the first word or brushstroke, a new meeting: how many little fears to be dispelled with courage of the soul!"

Norma Blackwood

Lullaby

For hours today I waited in the house;
No sign of you or anybody else,
No rain outside or land, and even light
Was cut out or so it seemed as rooms
And beds all turned into previews
Of that room which all of us will know.

Now your head lies upon my arm:
I have the whole world in its crook,
Your breathing is the movement of the wind
Around the four corners and your pulse
The ebb and flow of tide, your hard frame
The rocky skeleton of Earth, and as
We rest, invisible cords bind us one
To one, tying us here and far beyond.

Robert Gurry-Zentner

Madonna's Cloak

(for Gabby, whose idea it was)

Love is the longest and most enduring thread of all.
Take the deep love that bonds parent and child.
You'll find a cord that can never be cut or snapped:
an umbilical of infinite elasticity, more pliable than gold.
When your child grows to travel
it will stretch around the globe.
Anyone who crosses between
never can sever this thread.
Rather they gather it round their middle,
pulling it along ever after.
So enmeshed with the weft and warp
of interconnections has the world become,
it is now wrapped in an intricate weave of lovely twine
like a warm woolly blanket that will last
Mother Earth for all of time.

Barry Dean

Strands

(Sidbury 1993)

Washing my hair
I think of her
sitting on the door-stoop
hair gleaming in the pale sun
as she listens to the baying of hounds,
dreams of the young squire
doffing his cap
as he rides by in his red coat.

Her fate
a tumble in the hay
with one of the village lads
under the harvest moon,
feeling the weight of his body,
on bad days the weight of his hand.

In the spring
the quickening
fields of yellow daisies,
foxgloves among the hedgerows
and the child in her womb.

Wind stirs the white daisies
that grow among the slanted tombstones,
names obliterated by the wind and rain.
Does she lie there with her children?
Out of sixteen only two survived.

I think of her
cooking griddlecakes on the smoking hob,
fetching water form the well,
helping out at the great house,
binding the sheaves after harvest.
Our lives linked by strands
that stretch back 500 years.

Hilarie Lindsay

Covering the Distance

it is winter
I am cold
the deep V of arms grown cold
with holding
hold me

life's map is visible here
in distinct hills

a woman wrings water from knotted sheets

mucks out a cow bail

shucks the marrow from cane

in-grown calluses
protect her from wildfire.

Pat Pillai

Biding Time

(Arthur reads a book. After a few seconds, just as he turns a page a business card falls on the floor. Arthur picks it up, examines the card…he then picks up a phone receiver and dials a number.)

Arthur:
Good evening. Can I have extension 735? Thank you…Hello. Good evening. May I talk to…? Pardon? Is it 735? Well I'd like to…I'd like…I'm sorry. Can you put me back to the switchboard? Excuse me Madame, but I wanted Extension 735 and there is some woman…Er...yes…I see…Er…Thank you. So can you connect me with 753 then? Thanks. *(Pause)* Good evening. May I talk to God? Oh. That's you. Oh. Is that really you? Well I was flipping through the Bible and I found this card. Yes. Uh huh. I'm sorry to bother you. I have no idea. No…I don't know what's happened! That's why I'm calling. To find out. Why can't you help me? I don't know. I think I'm still alive. Why shouldn't I be? Well, I'm a bit dizzy… yes…but it's happened to me before. Quite often. Why? I thought it was a great opportunity…I always had so many questions…so I'd like to have a chat, a little talk without a middleman being involved…A middleman? A priest…or a monk… rabbi…What do you mean you don't know…? You're kidding. A priest is a man who represents you…How do you mean…well, a kind of an agent…I don't know how to describe…The point is that everyone knows what a priest is… and you…How come? You see there is, for instance, a religion that claims that you…no…there are many religions…You don't know?! This is really ridiculous. Have you heard the word BIBLE? Tora…Koran…You must be joking…Bestsellers…the most successful books…that's what it means. Religion is the form of worshipping you. Yes. Because people believe in you.

No, not everybody, but there is a quite significant number who do. And they do it in various ways. Yes and that's why they need religions. Yes...No. Don't you really? Well how can I explain it. No, I'm sorry. I won't take much of...well, I have only one question. Did you or did you not create the whole universe and us? Well that's what people believe. Yes. And that you are taking care of...hang on...just wait a minute. I don't want to annoy you – I just want to know. You see, I personally came to the conclusion that people created you. They needed you so they invented you. It's like theatre, art, philosophy. Yes that's what I thought. And I was deeply convinced that you were a product of someone's imagination but now since I've been talking to you my theory of your existence has gone...Because I'm talking to you. We're having a chat, aren't we? Blah blah blah blah. I tell you honestly, I'm actually glad that nobody is witnessing our conversation. Why? Because if someone witnessed me talking to you on the phone the way I am, they would first think that I am mad, or that for some dubious reason I'm pretending to talk to you. What a question...why! Because others talk to you only through prayers, ceremonies, rituals... not on the bloody phone...Well nobody talks to you on the phone. Some actually pretend that they don't talk to you at all, so they whisper their requests in total seclusion or they yell out things like "God help me", "Oh God", "Oh God bless you". Why are you laughing? What's so funny about it? No. I'm sorry. But the real question is: did you or didn't you create the universe and us? Yes I can understand that but...OK. Well, another question. Are you eternal or...OK I'm listening...Yes. And then what? Yes. So how did you do it...? This is incredible. That simple. I'm speechless. It's unbelievable. It's so logical...almost primitive. God. You see, our perception, I mean our human perception is created in a completely different way. Yes. I understand it. But the problem is that people have gone in the absolutely opposite direction...they interpret the whole thing so differently. There are some who totally exclude your involvement but the majority believe it was you…but nobody ever thought that it was done the way you just described. Well I'm totally convinced, but there's no way I can explain it to others…no…no way. Well there were even theories that we actually don't exist…Yes…and what we think exists is just a projection, an illusion dreamt by only one of us. The problem is that every single person thinks that he is the one who is the one. So we really have no answer. Well, but what you told me is just incredible. That simple…You did what, sorry? Really? Well I'm very sorry but I personally find it a bit unfair. Yes, because if you really did it that way, and then you…OK I'm listening. Well some people believe that you interfere in various ways, like through your son for instance. Pardon? Your son. Didn't you hear about it? Well…you don't know much, do you? Your son. What do you mean? I wouldn't say so. But people don't know. They still believe he was your son. Are you kidding? Wait a minute…You really want me to go and say that this son of yours was a con man? I understand, but...Well, I'll be completely condemned. How shall I do it? Shall I say "Listen people, I had a chat with God and he asked me to tell you that his so-called son is a self-appointed con man"? Well he was finally executed. Yes. He was killed. Ironically I would become almost like him. Well he claimed that he spoke to you. No, not on the phone. I don't remember. It was a long time ago. I don't know…some spiritual devices. Yes. I really don't know. But he somehow managed to convince some people. I'm sorry, but I'm not prepared to follow his path. By the way, nobody would believe me anyway. Oh God!…Oh, nothing, you see, that's exactly what we say when we are in trouble. Yes. Oh God. Yes. Sure. It's only according to some religions. Well, there are some religions too. I don't know much about them. How should I know? Hundreds, thousands…You don't know what religion is? Religion is a form of worshipping you. Like…yes. Well sort of...You know what? I just can't believe that you are so ignorant. Many things. Yes. And they all believe it's true. Well, like, for instance, that you are divided into three or four or dozens...well some of them claim that son of yours is one of you. Oh come on...that's a dirty joke. Are you? So? You know nothing, eh? I'm sorry, don't think that I'm trying to be too familiar. But since I know how you created the world I feel...No, no, no, not less respect. More respect, actually. Of course. It's ingenious. That you are...I feel that you are a friend rather than...Yes. Because the way you speak to me is so casual...No. Really? After all this conversation I think it would be pointless to ask you whether hell and heaven exist. *(Pause)* Hell. H-E-double L. OK. Skip it. How do you know? Really? So this son of yours must be there too? No? So people don't join you there? Actually, where are you? What do you mean, you don't know? That's a good question. I don't know where I am either. That's the point. I have no idea where I am. Funny. I feel the same way. Only one person? One person out of the whole of humanity? But why? And who is that person? What did you just say? I...Well...No I'm fine. I'm sorry. What does she look like? No, I'm OK. Tell me what do you know about her? I can tell you. I know her. Or I knew her. No, I know her. Yes. Because in my universe, which is surrounded by the boundaries of my existence there was only one Maria. Well she died. By sheer accident. She was shot during the riots. Many people died there. But Maria died by pure chance. Ricochet. A bullet. Please don't interrupt. OK. Bullets are little pieces of metal designed to kill people. Yes. Well how should I know why people are killing other people – I don't know. I thought you'd tell me that. Obviously you can't. If you don't even know what death is. Yes, I understand. She died in my arms. How can I describe it? It was like she was falling into a deep sleep. She was very light, and then suddenly she became very heavy. And I loved her. I still do. What is love? Well you're asking such unexpected questions. And at such moments. Well people love you. No. Only those who believe in you. Oh all right. Love is…I don't know what it is. I knew it with Maria and this love has never been discussed, defined, verbalised. It just was there. So I'm not equipped enough, so to speak, to describe what it is. It was just…something…so how is she? No. Please. No. Because if I talked to her it would...no please…I believe that she exists. That she is still present near me. No. I just can't. Because if I hear her voice on the phone right now it would mean that she's gone forever. No. Look after her please…and don't tell her about this conversation, please. Do you understand? Do you really? Yes. You would if you understood what time is. Time. No I can't explain it. Our logic is very different. My logic relates to what I know. But you, being God, don't need to know anything. So we don't have mutual reference points. Even Maria…for you, she is an eternal something, whatever she is. For me she's associated with a sense of time and space, with our biding time...and that's how it should be, since I'm not capable of removing from my consciousness all the obstacles that created me and my personal world. I'm not even sure it's possible to become like you. Oh no, just a thought. Because some people say that man was created in God's likeness. But you are pure and ignorant. By the way, how come you speak English? All the languages? And what does it do to you? I mean language is knowledge. What? A device? Like a phone? What about dreams? Do you know that word? Dreams. Yes. A device too. Interesting. So do you really understand what I'm saying? No? So why do you pretend? Ahhh, I get you. So you know something? Well if you know I'm willing to communicate with you (laugh). Ahh – another device. I understand. So basically you don't care? So for you, time doesn't exist? But you understand the word, don't you? Another device, OK. So the world I'm in is de-fragmented and the order we adopted is just a pure illusion of order. I see.

Things that are happening after can happen before, though we don't like this. OK. I'll tell you something. I'm going to live in this undefined space and time for a while. I'm forced to occupy this something I'm practically in. No, it was great. I'm sincerely grateful. No, don't give me any advice please. Yes, I'm really happy. You know why? Because from now on, I don't have to believe in you, as others do. No. Because I know that you exist. What? No, I can't. It's impossible. Because nobody would believe me. And even if they did, they would all lose their faith. It would be a disaster. We cannot live without faith. Me? Yes it will be very difficult. But I have no choice now, have I? Of course I could...and then what? OK Let's say that I give this telephone number to my friend. And then he calls you. And then what? OK. And then he goes out and tells people about you. They would lock him up in a mental asylum. Let us say that we give this number to another eleven people...or to a dozen people…that would be better…then they would become a dangerous minority. They will be extinguished, just like that son of yours. Don't be upset, it's only an example, OK. And then some clever manipulators will establish a new religion to enslave people in some new form, new order, new frame...Hello? Oh you are there. No, it's all right. There was a funny noise… suspicious clicks. No, I don't think so. I don't think I will need to talk to you any more. Maria? No. I need to believe at least in her. Thank you, God.

(fragment)

Bogdan Koca

After Trakl: Christmas 2003

Humanity surrounds burning craters,
the drum roll of guns, footsteps on foreheads
of soldiers, the matte black steel of tanks.

Despair in the sunlight, in the light of a full moon,
broken grief and Eve's shadow.
The hunt, the blood money.

Light breaks through clouds onto the Lord's Supper.
The silence of bread and wine.
On the table, the off-white flesh of fish.

The twelve stand assembled.
Under olive trees at night they drink wine and cry out.
Saint Thomas lowers his hand into the wound.

Robert Adamson

Bringing Back a Melted Person

This lake is not water. It was a person with whom I spoke at length then he dissolved.

And I am not trying now to look at water, but rather I'm trying to recover a dissolved person. How do people become lakes like this which tree leaves and algae top?

Drop by drop, the dead descend on my door.

A boat stops for me under the sun.

And a wretched fit of trembling returns to sand.

I didn't shiver, but I went mad. The water is cold, but I didn't shiver. I just trembled a little. Then I went mad.

On the surface of the lake is a leaf. It was an eye. On the bank was a bough which was a human rib.

I try now to gather the leaves and boughs. I try to gather a person I loved.

But many have passed by here. They gathered leaves and firewood to kindle their hearths.

Gathering together a person will never happen. Gathering a complete set of limbs won't happen. Many of them were burned.

Nonetheless I must restore a person I loved. Loved ones must come back if you call them. They must come back even if they are water. If they are dead. If they are algae. Algae must become a human being when you summon it. And he will come, even if wet, if bloated, if rotten. It must come back a friend even if he died one thousand years ago.

There must be some way to gather people from the banks, a way to turn the leaves and boughs floating on lakes into human beings.

I didn't shiver. The limbs shivered. I had to plug the space between their joints in order to stop their shivers so they would still.

But how very protracted is the distance between joints!

I run slowly like the last drop of water which came down, and was too late to flow.

I run slowly scrambling to catch up with the running, and evaporate by and by.

I won't make it. Part of me will come to be in space and part of me will sink into the earth.

I'm late for my comrades and won't make it. I creep on but I won't make it.

Pieces of me I lose, pieces accompany me exhausted, and pieces become free-floating particles.

Even if I make it, which thing of me will make it?

Around me is grass and pebbles and dirt. Birds peck at part of me. Ants eat part of me. And part of me belongs to the grass and pebbles and dirt.

I run slowly, and above me rises a thread of me, and below me descends a thread of me. I run slowly between two needles stitching my nothingness.

I came down the last drop. I was in the cloud and came down. Am I looking for a person who dissolved or am I the one dissolving? Or have I, from searching so much for his dissolution, dissolved like him?

And I've come, instead of searching for him, to search for me!

I see on the way persons going by. Part of what remains of me sees persons.

These, most likely, haven't lost a person they love. Or they lost him and despite that are completing the way?!

I don't know how our legs don't stop walking when we lose a person we love. Weren't we walking, not on our feet, but on his? Wasn't the whole excursion for his sake? Wasn't he the excursion?

How can one walk if one's lost a person? I stopped. He was the one walking and I his follower. I was the one walking in him. When he stopped, I no longer had feet.

I'm late, creeping, and I'm evaporating. How then will I bring back a person who has dissolved? Mustn't I, more precisely, bring back myself first? Come back at least as a whole drop of water coming down on a leaf, on an eye, on a rib, on a shore?

Mustn't I, in order to extract a person from algae, be at least of lake water?

I'm late and I won't make it. All that I can do is see. I see from far-off. Distorted vision from the eye of a thing that is not cloud nor water nor solid nor vapour.

Then I don't see.

All of this is merely imagining. A glooming dark imploring glooming dark. I will not see and I won't make it and I won't restore a person and I won't bring him back...

I just am trying to creep along. I'm trying to catch up to my comrades.

But they've come to be far-off, very far-off.

Perhaps in the past I was a person searching for a person who had dissolved, or perhaps I was the one dissolving. Now not even a drop. And in my frightening identification between the water and vapour and the person, I search for a name with which to introduce myself when I meet the ants and grass and birds.

You are creeping like me. You will necessarily stop on a protrusion. Send out a cry to me from there, and I'll name myself with it.

Identifying between water and solid and vapour. Even so I have joints!

And there are empty places between my joints.

Waters crash into them. Winds crash into them and people crash into them.

Many people now traverse my joints. I don't know whence they come or whither they go. But they crash against my bones.

People I encountered once; people I encountered many times; people I have never encountered...but they gush out now, and bang on my bones.

I must open these bones so they may enter.

If only these bones were a door.

Whence have they come?!

I think that those we look at, enter our bodies via our eyes and become flesh and blood.

Some of them become some of those straying past between our joints and we continue thus hearing the raps on our bones.

I now hear water knocking.

I must open.

Wadih Sa'adeh
Translated from the Arabic by *Clarissa C. Burt*

Close

My father's body
come to the end of its use.
Forever his fineness is woven
into the flesh of my days.

Open

Soon I shall be sprung
into something definite.
Now I test the delicacy
of my freedom.

Ten Ch'in Ü

"My uncle works as a virgin."

Peter Cameron misheard when he said his eighty-six year old uncle worked as a verger.

'Tis easy
to be a virgin in seclusion.
How greater this virtue
in the midst of the world
and all its inclusion.

Christopher Bodame

"After the poem is tossed into the open, it is worried over and often overworked, but somehow in that first draft there is a knowing. How to describe that feeling? It's a bit like seeing something suddenly, as if for the first time."

Pat Pillai

If I Were Reinventing the Wheel

If I were inventing the wheel, it would be fast, fast as a flock
of pigeons flying in a joyful rush through the early morning
sunshine around a shallow orchard valley full of apple vapours
rising on the night dew up into the sky.

And it would have a beginning and an end so I could begin over
and over again.

If I were reinventing the wheel, it would be slippery, slippery as
an eel in the bottom of a bucket caught on a hook baited with
an earthworm dug up in my mother's garden on a gently sloping
hillside facing south. It would be perfectly round like the moon
once a month or distorted every so often as it wriggles about.

It I were reinventing the wheel it would be brown, brown as the stain on the inside of a teacup deposited by tea-leaves picked in Sri Lanka by a woman in her fifties who is skilled at choosing partners for the local village daughters though she herself only ever produced one son.

To quench my thirst I would circle my lips and tug gently at the surface tension.

And if I were reinventing the wheel, it would be as a rainbow falling from rain cloud and bouncing across sand dunes like a beach ball on its way to the office holding a takeaway coffee and a bagel with a piece bitten out.

If I were reinventing the wheel it would be as a squeaky beach singing in harmony with a blue mountain lake.

Or I could take the past where all histories gossip endlessly, and with a sharp blade and in one motion and in every probable direction with every possible option and every likely aim I would cut out a circle to describe where I've come from, why I live here and suggest where I am going and the likeness I could see there, I would procreate little circular problems which only I could solve.

But I haven't reinvented the wheel.

Instead I have invented muddied banks without jungles, railway trains without stations, I've invented climate change without a cycle. I've drawn treasure maps without titles, chased my tail around the bed, laid asphalt runways without end. Yet here at the wheel of my invention I rotate my likeness up hills and around corners and bring myself back to where it began to this place where I recognise friendship.

Ray Wittenberg

Eating Blood Plums

(for Pat)

Shearing's finished for the year.
Sheep graze in the paddock,
a white cockatoo lands in the plum tree,
ripe plums plop to the ground.
Sitting on the back step
we savour the bittersweet juice.

It's been a strange year he says
Brucellosis in the stud
and me with prostrate cancer.

Before my cataract operation I couldn't read.
Now I can see
but I've got no interest in the papers.
Get all I need from TV.

The old dog twitches,
he bends to stroke him,
Dreams he's chasing sheep.

Tiger the young terrier
rolls in the manure heap.

The poplars I planted are dying,
perhaps someone will replace them.

He points to the old yellow tractor.
Kath said I spent more time with it
than I did with her.

Her hydrangeas still bloom by the shed.

She used to pick them for the church at Christmas.
She's been dead three years.

I rise to leave. He hugs me.
Not many of my old friends left.
Waves as I turn out the gate.

The mountains blue on the horizon.

Hilarie Lindsay

Old friends

Like cloths washed together
whose colours have run,
you and I are now stained
in each other's dyes.

Ten Ch'in Ü

Where we are most active
is where we most rest:
in each other's hearts.

Christopher Bodame

Reunion in a Cemetery

Past rows of concrete headstones
along paths of white stained gravel,
they walk, past overgrown lawns
and weeping trees, and
drying bunches of flowers, little
brass cups and silver picture frames
with faded photographs.
They search, from memory, for the place
where Thomas is buried.

Once there were six of them,
inseparable at school: friends,
confidants, not yet lovers, set apart by their
friendship and shared coffees and smokes,
afternoons and nights.
The remaining five, only a year older,
move slowly forward not knowing what to expect,
glancing sideways at the dead,
the forgotten names.

Julie carries a picnic blanket over her shoulder
a cigarette in her fingers, puffing from habit,
youthful hair still glossy, cheeks still in bloom,
her eyes dark and sombre like pools in a cave.
One year on, she thinks, and still she doesn't know
where she's going, what she is going to be.
She brushes back strands of hair,
revealing earrings pierced into her ears.

Josh carries the drinks: whisky, gin, and vodka
and coke. He doesn't know what they drink anymore
so he just brought what he could find,
knowing they only drink the hard stuff.
His black curly hair not yet covering
the scar from the car accident of a year ago.
He rarely speaks now, and his laugh
when it comes, is silent and brief.

Becky, now overweight, is tiring badly,
puffing in shallow breath, thinking she wore
the wrong shoes for this, carrying the crisps
and the peanuts they will eat by the grave.
She wishes it would rain
so they could all go home.
She's not ready for this.

Luke carries a woollen woven satchel
over his shoulder. He hasn't told them he brought a
songbook and a book of poems to read,
perhaps for later, when they are ready to
accept Tom's death and move on, not to forget
but to face the world as it is now, and not what it was
when they were oh so much younger and so unaware
and so innocent.

Joanne, dressed in black as always, stumbles behind
carrying orange marigolds and white daisies she plucked
from her mother's garden on the way out the door,
rushing for the bus to get here on time.
She searches the graves, for a suitable cup to put
the flowers in, rehearsing in her mind the simple
ceremony she has planned. It's important to

have ritual, something to cleanse the wound,
to mark the moment as special.

Like strangers, they arrive separately at the grave.
The headstone no longer bright, just one of many.
Grass creeps over the bare edges, and the shade
of a eucalypt in the late afternoon
already darkens the stone.
The sun rolls off the sky towards Africa.
They stare at the engraved stone, the fatal last
date etched there, somehow so long ago and so final.
Juliet spreads the blanket.

"Hi Tom," says Luke, and the rest smile shyly.
Joanne places the flowers gently beneath his name.
They slump round the blanket, a place for Tom at the end.
Luke pours drinks, and places one next to
the flowers. They sip in silence, the liquor
warming their tight throats and carrying away
the sigh, the awkwardness, the held back tear.

Becky turns away, toward the sunset, raising her arms
her hands outstretched, fingers quivering,
and they all join hands, a chain of memory passing
through them. "This is good, we can do this," she says.
Overhead, sparrows race for home, and far off
the dull roaring of the freeway continues
as people head for home, from another day.

John Weerden

Road to Florence

Trees hold their breath –
their last leaves ready to fly
with the first wind gust.

An old house, rust coloured,
floats by the road:
a ghost out of the grey mist.

Hilarie Lindsay

Essoyes

Forty-four leagues southeast of the grand Notre-Dame
the Saint-Rémy cathedral still dominates the village on its own scale,
its pointed towers like stakes driven into the earth by God
to mark his claim on these few hundred souls.
From the Loches bridge, a silo now squats
like an Op-Art chafer beetle at the gates of the cemetery
where cypress, willow and the flowering rushes of the riverbank
cradle our ancestors' bones. Will I ever dare
to make that rustic pilgrimage to the country of my spring,
see my memories blighted like the rhythms and contours
of all the surrounds, the old house slipping into decay,
home to rats, dormice and spiders; and all those images
of a youth spent in comfort and shelter that I took
for granted? Will I be able to retrace that long path
to the wellsprings of my heart? Essoyes...
in a backyard run wild, at the other end of the world
strangled by lantanas, I haven't breath enough
to whisper your name.

Telly Nakhjavani-Hall
Translated from the French by *John Carey*

Dreams

1

She wakes up
with a bird in her mouth
a white bird breaking through the clouds at dawn
I'll shoot some photographs tonight
she says
before going back
to sleep.

2

Last night I saw Fidel
a friend of mine who shot himself
a couple of years back.

He was a whirlwind
dancing, breaking through a rhythm
of shadows, sounds and lights
then suddenly
he stopped
and kept
        the most perfect equilibrium
        as if evoking a motionless hawk.

I threw a small stone at his face;
he didn't change his position but
quietly and brightly smiled at me.

Mario Licon Cabrera

Maternal Doubt

It will come, an informed sneak thief
On a drowsy hot day; it will quietly
Wait in verandah shade, ready to prey;
It will stand like the clay pots Mother gave,
Linking three generations of women living
With giving a fine salmon pink geranium.

It will feed on fear, that I have not blessed
His charm and excess with patience enough,
That tears may mark his heart not just
His mother's eyes, tired from care walking
Through dark open doors, empty bed
At four. A future nagging to know 'Where?'

It will harp, like the voice I disown, as I
Wrestle at midday a drugged giant from sleep,
Forcing his angel to face my confused
Reasoning, and wrath. The morning
My own, I have gathered to my breast
A stark courage called maternal love.

It will drum in a mind that sits idle,
While needle and thread firm into shape
A hat to wear once, to fit a fancy notion
That appearances count, or can ever cover
What was not tended at ten, or twenty,
Or two, wondering if and what can undo.

It will drown when I wake to hear metal
Pound metal, its echo meeting rock, deep
Rivers of laughter ringing from father
To son, to fly far up the valley, new
Fencing announced, their bond
Resounding where earth meets sky.

It will mend, with rain that softens the earth
Whose roots remember last spring
His kindly hands planting leeks and lettuce, lush
Leaves of sweet beet, in the hope he may lust
After such simple things while walking
Through avenues of dark suits to new worth.

Joanna Millicer Hempel

Sons

He said *You never sit and sew like Mother did.*
How could he know the hours she spends,
playing Penelope to his Ulysses,
turning collars, sewing patches,
with her son by her side,
listening for unsteady footsteps on the stairs,
while grease congealed around the leg of lamb.

Hilarie Lindsay

I the answer
ask the question
and feign confusion.

Christopher Bodame

Life there

There she buried
her child, and waited
to lie beside him for years.
When finally
they lowered her down
into that soil,
she was only one day old
while he was already an old man.

Wadih Sa'adeh
Translated from the Arabic by *Sargon Boulous*

Another herb

Opium is the herb of the other isthmus
drop by drop they drink their delusions.
Intoxicated by waking
lightning becomes
ashes in their hands.

Shawki Moslemani
Translated from the Arabic **Papers of Solitude**
by *Raghid Nahhas* and *Noel Abdulahad*

Young Children and Old People

Old people have no time left but they have all the time in the world.
Young children have no sense of time at all.
When mothers yell out to their children to come in, it's time for tea,
Their children invariably reply:
"It can't be tea-time yet, Mum, we're having too much fun,"
Which goes to show that children either have a well-developed sense of logic
Or no sense of logic at all which is why reason never works with children.
Threats work so much better.
Children understand power.
They know that those horrible grizzly fairytales tell the truth:
Grown-ups eat children.
They know,
They can see the truth of it in your eyes
When you look at them like that
And anyway, Granddad says so.
(Granddad's getting his revenge for your putting him in the old
persons' home.)

Darryl Reid

Vanishing

The land has become flat, and the riverbanks
are low and further away.
My mother's world is vanishing behind her:
each day a piece of her world,
once so complete, disappears,
unable to be retrieved,
in a time which now fragments.
Fate's new world, so strange and unfamiliar,
and incompatible, belongs to others.
Change now is simply loss, things just slip away,
sometimes noticed, sometimes not.
Familiar sounds, familiar places, familiar faces,
going, going, irretrievable.
Each day they fall away, bit by bit,
as her world disappears behind her.
The sense of loss saddens and all that's left
is shadows lengthening, the memories floating
on a broadening river.
Each day the physical inconvenience of pain
that lasts and lasts, and the thought of what's to come,
masks the cutting away.
The journey has been long and memories
stretch behind in a wake of foam and waves
that once parted now come together, glittering.
Year by year, how sweet the memories.

John Weerden

"Old age is not for the faint-hearted."

Heather Weerden

Beachcombing

Where the waves flop and sag
a world's dead gather. Molluscs drag
their gravestones to the cemetery
and collapse. Scraps of algae
and seaweed wreathe them; fish come
in dying ripples, dying. Scum
of earth and water tries to bury moccasins
and sandals, driftwood and baked-bean tins
in vain, but lays them out brown, green,
ochre and rust-red, like fragments seen
in masons' yards. Nothing shocks
the eye with levity, splashes rocks
and sand with stubborn textures, tints
that won't compromise. Nothing? Here, there, glints
of a whiteness whiter than bones, than chalk,
than newsprint, whiter than white, stalk
the beach, like Robespierre, incorruptibly.
No decay and change within, without: no sea
corrodes the confidence of hard-flexed
carbon chains of inbuilt whiteness unannexed
by water, earth or sky –
immortal monument to ICI.

David Tribe

"I am looking for a piece of land with magic."
Marjolyn Gluyas

Reflections

Asfumana
Luxiein
Asdrubama
Solfix
Adie ex in urxas

It was AsDualAl who one night in the shape of a bird
printed with his beak this mantra on my chest.

"Don't look at the whole moon of the mirror,
only at a shard of it, nothing more than that
especially if you are always amongst others...
Be careful, don't smash that shard, leave it outside
just before closing your doors."

Mario Licon Cabrera

"*Asfumana, Luxiein, nervatures*: these are made words."
Mario Licon Cabrera

"Everything that enables our younger generations in Cape York Peninsular to achieve their fullest potential, talent and creativity so that they have the confidence and capacity to orbit between two worlds and enjoy the best of both."

Noel Pearson

in his Judith Wright Memorial Lecture at **Ngara** the 4th Australian Poetry Festival on 5th September 2004 at Balmain Town Hall, addressing the question,"What, if anything, might Aboriginal people wish to take from the various settler cultures?"

field

"The place where the current from the past and the current from the future overlap is the human body and the region of overlap is the domain of consciousness."

Robert Sardello
'Love and the world'

"It is never too late to be what you might have been."

George Eliot

Las Meniñas

Where we are standing is timeless. If I open
This brilliant portal of his mind, a courtier
Excluded but admiring, I can watch
Crowds pour across his canvas from the past
And into the future as he goes on painting
Our world in which he seems to recognise
More grown-up children, more Velásquez faces:
And here our other selves to infinity
Disclose the things they too have heard about us.

John Miles

Beaches at dusk

Remember the beaches where we walked at dusk?
We watched the sun fall into the ocean,
dived around each other's bodies, smooth as seals,
foam lingering on our skin.
We walked in each other's footsteps
as the holes slowly filled with water,
trusting in the half-light,
trying to hear each other's hearts
speak their different languages.
The seagulls seemed to have no trouble.
Did we expect them to translate for us?

Pip Griffin

National Park, Audley

inhospitable arched carvings tower above us_
beside the river whose swinging hair holds bones
leaves rattle and shiver into autumn
we are pulled down into dark places underwater

and the river speaks

I am ancient
before old
your fires cannot destroy me

this is my place

acerbic accents rise from the river flats
a baseball bat swings wide disturbing young cricketers
playing on our willow patterned picnic

tourists

the sneer rises   unvoiced
as cockatoos backflip words into silence
we watch as they screech northward
toward hillsides of flowering gums which
having survived summer
expire statements in blue vapour

and this place lets us in

Pat Pillai

Entrances

You never quite know what is
there, it's just a matter of

beginning once again...
This heat can make your mind

opaque, yet there is this
inwardness of things that calls

for more attentiveness;
so I'm learning how to be here.

Every day becomes a door
into the inside — of this house

of light, the shadowed pool,
the intimate immensity of trees.

Or into what is held between us
in a place where the real

learning asks insistent questions.
Outside, the dirt road

empties in the dusk and at last
the dust settles, as night

folds up into its own. Ah,
they are so demanding, these

collaborations of silence
calling out beneath the world.

John Allison

Archaic Torso of Apollo

Rainer Maria Rilke

We never saw his magnificent head,
therein the eyes grew to maturity. But
his torso glows yet like a candelabrum,
in which his presence, but now turned down,

endures and shines. Or else that arch of breast
could not bedazzle you, and in the subtle
turning of the loins no gentle smile could go
toward that middle which procreation bore.

Or else this stone would stand disfigured and short
under the shoulder's transparent descent
and glimmer not like coat of preying beast;

and wouldn't thus break forth from all its margins
like a star: for there is nowhere a place
which sees you not. You have to change your life.

Translated from the German by *Manfred Beck*

Someone

someone is having a morning coffee
someone is typing up an email letter to send somewhere
someone is glancing out the window at the blue september sky
someone is doing something
someone is faxing something somewhere
someone is receiving a phone call from someone else
someone is dialling a number but that number is busy
someone is going to the toilet
someone is doing something
someone is walking upstairs for an exercise
someone has chosen the lift
someone is going down
someone is coming up
someone is opening a large parcel containing poetry submissions
someone is writing a rejection letter to a novelist
someone is thinking of someone else
someone is doing something
someone is having a little hangover
someone is chatting on the side
someone's mobile phone is ringing
someone's laptop has just crashed
someone is restarting
someone is getting technical support and listening to the recorded
messages
someone is running whose high-heels are being heard
someone is turning his head
someone is having fun
someone is approaching 50
someone is approaching 23
someone is doing something
someone is going to have a smoko outside the building
someone is worried about his marriage
someone is looking forward to her upcoming wedding ceremony

someone is alive
someone is doing something
someone misses yesterday's fish
someone is checking and rechecking a large sum of money
someone is having a meeting
someone is listening to birds singing on his dvd
someone is pouring tea into her pot of frangipani
someone is doing something
someone is looking at his screen
someone is stretching his legs and arms
someone is a little unhappy about a difficult client
someone has just lost in the stock market through a lack of sleep

someone turns his head to see the enormous head of an airplane
        near his window
someone is meeting someone

Ouyang Yu

Yesterday's Morning

Again, that yet unnamed bird,
that breaking of silence into
a new restart for the things to be –
once again renamed. Meanwhile,
with a mute flap the song flies away.

Mario Licon Cabrera

Among You

A coppersmith
    hammers in my head.
A painter
    colours my eyes.
A mad man
    emerges from me.
And another
    knocks to get in.

So I ask you O judges
    do not call me *you*...
I am a multitude
    and do not know all my clan
    including the criminal.

Once you sentence me
    the culprit shows up
    among you.

Shawki Moslemani
Translated from the Arabic **Where the Wolf is**
by *Noel Abdulahad* and *Raghid Nahhas*

In the Bungle Bungles

I am 73.
My body is
bleached and parched by the sun
blown by the wind
bitten by beasties
scratched by pricklies
shaken and rattled by rough rocks.

I climb over ledges
wade in knee-deep sands
through creeks in dark caves.

I erect my tent each evening
dismantle it each morning.

I swim with crocodiles
play with black children
admire the sun rising
and the sun setting
day after day.

I belong to the moon and the stars each night.
I feel truly alive at two in the morning
in the light of the half moon.

Susan Haris

To sing is not to sing a song
But to listen and to hear.

Christopher Bodame

The Sound of Alone

one dog's bark detaches itself from the distance
the wind snuffles through dry leaves and runs off
my carrot grater becomes a loud instrument
and each semibreve
a morning festooned with spider silk
where silence
is as breath

Pat Pillai

Hippeastrum

I picture you gathering them,
saffron powders on your shirt and
nose. You bring them to me,
nodding in a bucket.

They brim my blue St Vinnie's vase.
When I draw one out,
so much water pours
from the stem.

Ten Ch'in Ü

My mother's balcony

Shadows, breezes, tangles of adventurous jasmine
and especially the sun like to park here
where she again lays out grains, bread and water.

Visitors to the meeting serenely presided over by
music from an old radio are respectful, not jostling
over the morning bath or breakfast.

Among them, a cockatiel which perches on her shoulder.
They say he's confused for he calls his nest by her name
yet all rejoice her return, daily check on her progress.

The loneliness of sterile hospital bed now banished
to memory as they surround her (she with voice
ransacked by that illness) with song.

Here an oasis prohibits confusion and disappointment,
invokes paradisiacal forest, clear lakes, light
(things are shadows, snapshots of infinite worlds).
This narrow balcony accommodates many;
together they speak a language coherent with love.

One afternoon I see a green budding on the balcony.
I know a bird carries a mustard seed in his beak:
a gift from the north of the north
to the south of the south.
The mustard is no longer imprisoned in the Holy Books.

Anis Ghanem
Translated from the Arabic with *Ten Ch'in Ü* and *Ann Davis*

Body and Consciousness: a Double Take

Steven Guth was invited to write a piece and afterward *Robert Sardello* was asked to respond to the view. *Steven* has the first and last word while *Robert* has more lines in this double bill.

The esoteric information, the Spiritual Science that was written last century, is based on scientific concepts that were coined in the 1880's. We struggle with this as words gain modern meanings often far removed from the concepts which created them in the first place. An example is the word, *will*: when Blavatsky referred to this in 'Isis Unveiled' (Vol 1 pg 144) she used it to describe a hypnotist's thought "transversing space, penetrating the pores of another individual and superseding his own facilities and forcing him to a predetermined action".

Nowadays in this age of personal development *will* is seen as something that only comes from our own, inner mental processing and directs our movements so that we can, say, light a cigarette. Blavatsky's *will* was clearly separate from *thinking* and *feeling* while ours isn't - we feel a need for a cigarette and we think about what it means to our health.

I think it is time to look at our esoteric terms and descriptions and align them to modern ideas. Computers have given us new ways of describing mental processes. Recent brain research tells us that we have no consciousness area in the brain, consciousness seems to be a process (see Susan Greenfield's 'The Human Brain'). Recent astronomical discoveries tell us that there are other planets out there in other solar systems so planet life and even quasi humans may not be unique in a cosmos of billions upon billons of solar systems.

Since reading the Rudolf Steiner lecture of 15th Nov 1917 usually entitled in English 'Geographic Medicine' twenty years ago I have been very aware that Freud's idea of the unconscious could be extended with Steiner's insights into an entity he called the *double* that enters our body before birth. Over the years I have given much thought to how this double works and how to describe the probable mechanisms involved. The best explanation that I have come up with uses new ideas and new terminology.

However, when I present the subject to any group I always start with two of Steiner's illustrations from the Goetheanum windows. Steiner undoubtedly understood the double. The first is the central image of the green window in the north titled *The world develops the will.* It is a snake with a semi-human head and seven chakra points along the way. It is being blessed by a human sitting on a rock. This is the double, the energy of the spine with its myopic stare. Steiner has represented what I see as the antenna aspect of the chakras with little wings. The second illustration is the central rose-coloured window in the south titled *The world develops.* In it a human form gives rise to the face of wisdom at the end of a rainbow which expands into the realm of the moon and the the stars. This is the higher self released during contemplation or sleep.

I see that we have two processing systems in our bodies. A spine with its antenna tuned to earthly life processes. The spine brain is what gives rise to the double. Our higher self finds its home in the cortex of our brains, our head mind receives and sends information which is shared throughout the galaxy.

In this model chakras can be described as location in the spine's mind tuned to send and receive specific wavelengths. (Philip Callahan's 'Tuning in to Nature' shows that insects read wave patterns with systems that are similar to TV antennas and to our spines.) And I suggest that our skull with its cortex can be considered a dish antenna tuned into receiving signals from galactic space.

Consciousness is the process that appears in our mind like words on a computer screen, a mixture of the double and cosmic higher self information. We process information that comes from the physical world through our senses as well as information that comes from the spiritual worlds into our skulls. Our bodies belong to the earth but we are really devas, shining beings, consciousness in action - we belong to the cosmos.

When we sleep we naturally travel into the cosmic, galactic spheres, and we wake up refreshed. We do this after death too. We are only really alive when we die. The secret of meditation is that it lets us put our double, and our senses, to sleep so we can access our higher self and through it the spiritual spheres.

It is not rare for the higher self aspect of human consciousness to become locked out of using the human brain successfully. The result is an unbalanced processing of consciousness within the human personality. The spine brain, the double, takes over dominance of consciousness processing within the human. It is common to see this in people who have been drug, medicine or chemical damaged. It also happens with senility which is the gradual shutting down of higher self contact. Memories remain but new information cannot be processed. Creativity is gone, habit patterns continue and even they slowly fade as they are replayed over and over.

Steven Guth

I greatly appreciate Steven's work of updating the language of Spiritual Science. It is a noble effort, an attempt to speak with those who might have difficulty understanding Rudolf Steiner. Such updating has to be done by working with contemporary concepts to understand the spiritual forces working within them as well as taking extreme care not to replace vivid descriptions by abstract and inadequate terms. For example, while the term 'information' is certainly contemporary, readers will have to work inwardly to determine whether it is accurate to describe the relation of the body, the cosmos, and the mind as transfers of information. Here, a highly materialistic term is being used to replace descriptions not just of processes, but the action of spiritual beings. The question is: are the spiritual beings involved in what goes on spiritually between self and cosmos the same ones that are involved in the transfer of information? If not, the updating of language has also reduced a spiritual occurrence to another sort of event.

To say that recent brain science now states that we have no consciousness in the area of the brain is an odd sort of update, for this was known, in detail, by the esoteric anatomists of the 15th century and earlier. Robert Fludd is particularly good on this point. He, along with many others, including Hildegard of Bingen at a different time, viewed the activities nowadays attributed to the brain such as sensing, imagining, and thinking, as occurring at the place of the ventricles, the hollow spaces of the brain. There are seven ventricles of the brain according to the esoteric anatomists, though contemporary science knows only four. Blavatsky too, describes the functions of sensing, imagining, and thinking as occurring at the site of the ventricles. They did so, first of all, based upon their abilities to see clairvoyantly and thus describe the actual processes rather than theorize about them. And, they struggled mightily with how the human body could be both a material thing and a spiritual presence.

The spiritual cosmos is not *out there* in space, millions of miles away, so here again, we have to be careful in transferring spiritual understandings of cosmic forces as beaming in from space as if some material force comes light years from the planets into the human body.

In 'A Psychology of Body, Soul, and Spirit' (Anthroposophic Press: Hudson NY 1999, updated from the German text), Rudolf Steiner describes the forces, the currents involved in the forming of the human body. The human body is much more than an information receiving centre with the skull functioning as a 'dish antenna'. Such a notion, while having the merit of utilizing concepts that can be readily understood in our time, unfortunately also reduces the true mystery of the human body. Steiner describes three polarities of currents that are forming the body: the I-being—Astral body current; the physical body—etheric body current; and the sensation body—feeling soul current. The physical body results from the coming together of these currents, and where they come together there is a kind of damming up of currents that results in the appearance of the human body. The human body is a convergence of spiritual worlds, elemental worlds, sun forces, material forces, soul and sense forces. And those forces are the actions of spiritual beings. What an extraordinarily beautiful picture! And, one that is highly instructive on how to live as embodied spirits. A picture filled with awe, reverence and wisdom which is, at the same time, what we can aspire to in order to be true to the being of our body.

Steiner gives us here a highly important imagination. One that, incidentally, is spoken of in the language of forces and currents, which is far more contemporary than the language of information. Modern physics has no trouble whatsoever understanding this kind of description. Further, the language of forces and currents brings about a re-imagining of the body. What we speak of and experience as our body has the characteristic of being a solid 'thing' because, since the late 15th century, the imagination of the body has been formed by anatomy and physiology. In other words, our taken-for-granted imagination of the human body is that of the corpse. Steiner's description goes a very long way in pushing us toward an imagination of the body as the converging of worlds, the converging of spiritual beings. I suppose that Steven would speak of such a convergence as complex information, received by the cortex and the spine. Steiner, of course, was familiar with that kind of language too. And appreciated it. But, he never confused where the currents and forces were reflected with the activity itself. He understood that the activity is primary and that thinking, feeling, and imagining had to go in the direction of our developing the capacities to experience the activity.

In the same book, which is really the book that can serve as a foundation for a true spiritual psychology, Steiner also gives a description of the activity of consciousness. It is something far more than, other than, "the process that appears in our minds like words on a computer screen, a mixture of the double and cosmic higher self information" interacting. Steiner describes two time currents – a current, which we are all familiar with, one that runs from the past to the present and toward the future, and another current that runs from the future into the present and into the past. An astounding imagination! And one that is true and quite easy to verify for oneself. The future is present with us as hope, wanting, wishing, expecting, longing, and indeed, intuiting something as here when it cannot be seen. All of our science and indeed all of contemporary understanding is based only on the notion of time running from past toward future. Then, esotericists and mythologists sometimes add a notion of timelessness.

Consciousness is a particular time experience. Not an experience of time, but the human being as a time being. Consciousness is the region of overlap of the time current from the future with the time current from the past. That place of overlap is the human body. That place of overlap is also the place where a vertical current, the I-being enters, for while consciousness can be accounted for by the two time currents, the particular way in which, at times, there is the experience not just of consciousness, but of an I-consciousness, cannot be understood in terms of the two time streams. Nor can it be understood in any material terms. This consciousness enters around two years of age, without instruction from anyone.

Steiner's description of consciousness is revolutionary! It is not Steiner who needs to be updated but rather the rather hopeless literalised consciousness that characterizes current simple science (I make here the important distinction between those who operate out of a 19th century notion of science and truly creative science. 'Simple science' refers to the former) that needs updating. When the updated language of information theory is used to describe the activity of the human body, it is inevitable to come to the kind of imagination of aging that Steven speaks of when he says: "In senility memories remain but new information cannot be processed. Creativity is gone, habit patterns continue and even they slowly fade as they are replayed again and again." He goes on to say that senility is "the gradual shutting down of higher self contact." The imagination he provides of this process is exactly that provided by contemporary science which has led to putting older people either in places that are akin to perpetual cruise ships or giant warehouses.

When viewed through spiritual science, aging has an entirely new meaning. The sometimes incomprehensible speaking and behaviour of some elderly people is due to the fact that they are already residing in the spiritual world. The memories that seem to be repeated over and over again, when looked at with careful observation are moments in their lives that were true destiny moments; that is, moments when the future announced itself. Now, that future has come. Of course, it is true, we don't know how to listen. If we listen through the concepts of materialism, the spiritual voice of the aging can never be heard.

We are faced with an information age, perhaps not to update what we know into that terminology and those concepts, but precisely so that we can work against this most pervasive materialism. Not by opposing it, for it has much to offer. But work against it by developing the capacities to truly perceive the world-currents. This development comes about, not in opposition, but as a reverse ritual. Taking materialistic notions and going the other way with them, reversing them. Taking them into the spiritual world. I am certain that is Steven's intention.

Robert Sardello

My conception of consciousness tends to fit into the Buddhist framework. I see my consciousness, our consciousness as part of all consciousness.

> "Know that your mind itself is immeasurable, the container of a myriad, myriad universes, each of them vast beyond your comprehension. All the illimitable power that exists in those myriads of universes would be yours in full, if you had the wisdom enough to use it. The same is true of every sentient

being...when a single bee sucks honey, all beings in the myriad universes suck honey; when a worm is crushed, all beings in those universes are crushed. Remember, the source of all power lies within yourself." *John Blofeld*

'The Bodhisattva of Compassion' Shambhala, Colorado 1987

I think Steiner was saying just this: that all consciousness is interrelated in the universe. But he had to use the German conceptual frameworks of his time. I have also come to understand that consciousness travels outside time: it is instantaneous within the galaxy, within the cosmos. So the idea of *out there* is not linked to modern ideas associated with the speed of light.

Essentially I read what Robert says in his fourth paragraph as expressing what I said but in more complex language and from a somewhat postmodern anthroposophical viewpoint.

I also think that Robert's description of Steiner's insights is remarkably similar to what Australian Aboriginals express as the need for human involvement in 'The Dreaming' which is to them how the world *develops*. Within their cultural framework, it is their being, their living, their *doing* that enables the past to flow into the future and future to manifest in the present.

Consider a ten-year old nomadic boy in a tent. He is in the Iranian desert with a carpet frame in front of him, adding knots, one by one, into his family's traditional pattern. With each knot he takes the family's heritage and moves it into the future. He, by being the future, is the way the family will move into the future...children are taught this by being, by *doing*. The boy arrives to work the future into the present - the present is the fulcrum point of the future.

Steven Guth

Robert Sardello: 'Love and the World' Lindisfarne Books 2001
http://www.sophiajournal.org http://www.spiritualschool.org
Steven Guth: http://www.kheper.net/ecognosis

Joys

Spit on a whetstone
and in circles slowly
hone an old pocketknife.

With a stick beat
branches so that fruit
falls unbruised on cushioning grasses.

Take freshly pulled onions
and plait.
Hang them in a shed
to sharpen.

Dig potatoes.
Shake soil
from the garden fork tines
discovering universes
of stellar orbs.

Weed between the rows of mint
until bruised leaves
scent enough to drunken.

Using a pestle squash
new picked tomatoes
into basil.

With skill peel
a pippin apple.
The skin unbroken,
spirals continuously
from the blade.

Then bite
and the chilled sun
warms, revives.

These rituals
make our arguments
so little.

David Wansbrough

Who am I?
Li Bai

I'm a Blue Lotus – though not the monkish kind –
then too a scholar unemployed;
also an immortal spirit, in exile amongst men.
In taverns, tippling freely, I've spent some thirty
summers
and kept my name and fame well under wraps
(just like some occult text).
Oh District Lord of Hosts, why must you ask?
The living image of the incarnate Buddha,
the Golden Grain made flesh and blood again,
that's who I am !

Translated from the Chinese by *Rene Manning*

The rules

White gulls fly over
The moving ruff of reeds
and ducks glide on their upended doubles

the lake floats the park like a kite with tails

not balancing unwinding
a figure at the edge
not on holiday

lets it all fall

he undoes the sway
of plants over stillness   the lake's quietness
that birds can enter and leave

its surface holding the same
smoothness

to yell
an instruction
for the children

(they) must wait till later to eat (their) lunches

the class-room here's
too wide
for him

to encompass

Phyllis Perlstone

Field

"The works produced for this exhibition draw inspiration from Lake George, N.S.W. and King's Canyon, N.T.

A first platform of paint is laid according to the immediate colours, textures and forms of the situation. Later I develop this layer by realizing, or giving expression to, the emerging senses and responses often over a period of years. All this occurs in the paint itself. Language might arrive later.

The theme that particularly interests this work is that of landscape as a living field of being which inevitably tends towards the horizon, a new seasonal promise and the apparently vertical movement of the unconscious.

The sculptured heads are a tribute to the red sands that blow in every direction across the interior of the continent."

Peter Cameron on his March 2004 exhibition of abstract landscapes and sculpture from which the cover painting comes.

On the Edge

From a glance
fleeting from me
                    a crow flies away.
I go on cutting wood.

Shawki Moslemani
Translated from the Arabic **Where the Wolf is**
by *Noel Abdulahad* and *Raghid Nahhas*

Sitting in Front of a Mountain
Li Bai

A flock of birds in flight, high in the sky – they've gone!
A lonely wisp of cloud – loitering away…
That leaves only the mountain facing me:
We gaze at one another – neither of us wearying of the view.

Translated from the Chinese by *Rene Manning*

To Hölderlin
Rainer Maria Rilke

To linger, not even with the most familiar,
is given us; from out of the fulfilled
pictures, too suddenly the spirit plunges to further filling; seas
are first encountered in eternity. Here
falling is wisest. To fall out of the feeling mastered
down into the gleaned-at, onward.

For you, you magnificent one, for you, you conjurer,
the pressing image was a life entire, when you uttered it,
the line closed itself like destiny, a death itself
was in the gentlest, and you traversed it; but
the foregoing God guided you forth from yonder.

Oh you changing spirit, most changeable one! How they all do
live in the cozy poem, domestic, and long
remain within the narrow parallel. Partakers. *You only*
move through like the moon. And beneath lightens and darkens
herself your nightly one, the holy affrighted landscape,
which in departures you feel. No one
presented her more sublimely, gave her more wholly
back to the all, unneedy one. So too,

holy you played through years no longer reckoned,
with the unending joy, as though it *were* not within, lay
belonging to no one in earth's soft
lawns surrounding, abandoned by children divine.
Alas, what the greatest desire, you laid it, free from desire
stone upon stone: it stood. Yet even its toppling
bewildered you not.

What, though such an eternal one has been, mistrust we ever the
earthly still? 'Stead of learning in earnest
from the temporal, the feelings for what
future inclining in space?
Set out on the mountains of the heart. See there, how small,
see: the last village of words, and higher,
but again how small, yet one last
farmstead of feeling. Do you discern it?
Set out on the mountains of the heart. Stoneground
under our hands. Here too may some
things bloom; from a mute precipice
an unwitting herb singing blooms forth.
But the knowing one? Alas, he who began to know
and is silent now, set out on the mountains of the heart.
Much, with whole awareness, may go
about here, many a secure mountain animal
moves and lingers. And the great harboured bird
circles the peak's outright denial. –But
unharboured, here on the mountains of the heart?

Translated from the German by *Manfred Beck*

The Goldfinches of Baghdad

These finches are kept in gold-plated cages
and fruit boxes covered in wire mesh.
They are used by falcon trainers as lures
and rich patriarchs choose these living ornaments
to sing to them on their deathbeds. Their song is pure
and melodious. A goldfinch with a slashed throat
was the subject of a masterpiece painted by an artist
in the sixteenth century on the back of a highly polished
mother-of-pearl shell - it burns tonight in Baghdad,
along with the living, caged birds. Flesh and feathers,
hands and wings. Sirens wail, but the tongues
of poets and the beaks of goldfinches
burn. Those who cannot speak burn along with
the articulate, creatures oblivious to prayer burn
along with those who lament to their God. Falcons
on their silver chains, the children of the falcon trainer,
smother in the smoke of burning feathers and
human flesh. We sing or die. Singing death
as our songs feed the flame.

Robert Adamson

Contributors

Noel Abdulahad
Robert Adamson
John Allison
Neil Anderson
Antares
Robert Balas
Felicity Daphné Baldry
Manfred Beck
John Blackwood
Norma Blackwood
Christopher Bodame (Tof)
Sargon Boulus
Peter Bowden
Clarissa C. Burt
Jacqueline Buswell
Mario Licon Cabrera
Peter Cameron
John Carey
Assad Cina
Ann Davis
Barry Dean
David Joseph Deutch
Richard Deutch
Yvonne Deutch
Brook Emery
Luke Fischer
Cliff Forshaw
Danny Gardner
Anis Ghanem
Marjolyn Gluyas
Jacques Goldman
Sumie Goto
Pip Griffin
Robert Gurry-Zentner
Steven Guth
Telly Nakhdjavani-Hall
Miranda Su Lan Harding
Susan Haris
Joanna Millicer Hempel
Sue Hicks
Danu Huan Ho
Dhyan Tao-Li Ho
Ista Chuang-Yang Ho
Joanna Jaaniste
Vanajam Kaloo
Bruce Kirchoff
Bogdan Koca
Martin Langford
Hilarie Lindsay
Rene Manning
Paula McKay
John Miles
David Morris
Shawki Moslemani
Raghid Nahhas
John Pater
Phyllis Perlstone
Pat Pillai
Charles Plumridge
Josephine Porteus
David Pudney
Darryl Reid
Howard Roslington
Don Rowley
Jorie Manefield Ryan
Wadih Sa'adeh
Anton Sabella
Robert Sardello
Michael Sharkey
Margaret Smith
Irina Spinadel
Ten Ch'in Ü
Bill Tibben
David Tribe
Jaap van der Haar
Edilia Vidal-Porcu
David Wansbrough
Heather Weerden
John Weerden
Alan Whitehead
Susan Whitehead
Les Wicks
Ray Wittenberg
Dominique Yap
Ouyang Yu
Yuri (Hofsteters)
Jakob Ziguras